INTERVIEW
WITH A TYCOON

INTERVIEW WITH A TYCOON

BY

CARA COLTER

First published in Great Britain 2014
by Mills & Boon, an imprint of Harlequin (UK) Limited,
Large Print edition 2015
Eton House, 18-24 Paradise Road,
Richmond, Surrey, TW9 1SR

© 2014 Cara Colter

ISBN: 978-0-263-25589-8

Harlequin (UK) Limited's policy is to use papers that
are natural, renewable and recyclable products and made
from wood grown in sustainable forests. The logging
and manufacturing processes conform to the legal
environmental regulations of the country of origin.

Printed and bound in Great Britain
by CPI Antony Rowe, Chippenham, Wiltshire

To all those readers who come to visit me
on Facebook, thank you!

CHAPTER ONE

STACY MURPHY WALKER'S heart was beating way too fast. She wondered, gripping the steering wheel of her compact car tighter, how long a heart could beat this fast before it finally calmed itself out of pure exhaustion.

Or exploded, her mind, with its tendency to be overly imaginative, filled in helpfully.

But, still, she was entirely aware the slipping of her tires on the icy mountain roads was not solely responsible for the too-fast beating of her heart.

No, it was the sheer audacity of what she was doing.

Bearding the lion in his den.

A bronze name plaque, *McAllister*—in other words, the lion—set in a high stone fence, tasteful and easy to miss, told her she had arrived. Now what? She turned into the driveway but stopped before tackling the steep upward incline.

What was she going to say? *I need an inter-*

view with Kiernan McAllister to save my career as a business writer, so let me in?

She'd had two hours to think about this! No, more. It had been three days since a friend, Caroline, from her old job had called and told her, that amidst the rumors that his company was being sold, McAllister had slipped away to his Whistler retreat.

"This story is made for you, Stacy," her friend had whispered. "Landing it will set you up as the most desired business freelancer in all of Vancouver! And you deserve it. What happened to you here was very unfair. This is a story that needs your ability to get to the heart of things." There had been a pause, and then a sigh. "Imagine getting to the heart of *that* man."

Stacy had taken the address Caroline had provided while contemplating, not the heart of *that* man, because she was done with men after all, but the humiliating fact that what had happened to her was obviously the going topic in the coffee room.

But Caroline was right. To scoop the news of the sale of the company would be a career coup for a newly set loose freelancer. To lace that scoop with insight into the increasingly enigmatic McAllister would be icing on the cake.

But more, Stacy felt landing such an important article could be the beginning of her return, not just to professional respect, but to personal self-respect!

What had she thought? That she was just going to waltz up to millionaire Kiernan McAllister's Whistler cottage and knock at his door?

McAllister was the founder and CEO of the highly regarded and wildly successful Vancouver-based company McAllister Enterprises.

And what was her expectation? That he would open his door, personally? And why would he—who had once been the darling of the media and graced the cover of every magazine possible—grant an audience to her?

McAllister had not given a single interview since the death of his best friend and brother-in-law almost exactly a year ago in a skiing accident—in a place accessible only by helicopter—that had made worldwide headlines.

Now, Stacy hoped she could convince him that she was the best person to entrust his story to.

And here was the problem with imagination.

She could imagine the interview going so well, that at the end of it, she would tell him about her charity, and ask him…

She shook herself. "One thing at a time!"

It was a shot in the dark, after all. And speaking of dark, if she did not get her act together soon, she would be driving back down this road in the dark. The thought made her shudder. She had some vague awareness that ice got icier at night!

She inched forward. She was nearly there, and yet one obstacle remained. The driveway had not been plowed of snow, and the incline looked treacherous. It was in much worse shape than the public roads had been in, and those had been the worst roads Stacy had ever faced!

At the steepest part of the hill, just before it crested, her car hesitated. She was sure she heard it groan, or maybe that sound came from her own lips. For an alarming moment, with her car practically at a standstill, Stacy thought she was going to start sliding backward down the hill.

In a moment of pure panic, she pressed down, hard, on the gas pedal. The wheels spun, and in slow motion, her car twisted to one side. But then the tires found purchase, and as her car shot forward, she straightened the wheel. The car acted as if it had been launched from a canon and careened over that final crest of the hill.

"Oh, God," she exclaimed. "Too fast!"

She practically catapulted into the courtyard. The most beautiful house she had ever seen loomed in front of her, and she was a breath away from crashing into it!

She hammered on the brakes and yanked on her steering wheel.

She'd been on a ride at the midway once that felt just like this: the car spun like a top across the icy driveway. She bumped violently over a curb, flattened some shrubs and came to a stop so sudden her head bounced forward and smashed into the steering wheel.

Dazed, she looked up. She had come to rest against a concrete fountain. It tipped dangerously. The snow it was filled with fell with a quiet thump on the hood of her car.

She sat there in shock, the silence embracing her like that white cloud of snow on her hood that was obliterating her view. It was tempting to just sit and mull over her bad luck, but no, that was not in keeping with the "new" Stacy Walker.

"There's lots to be grateful for," she told herself sternly. "I'm warm, for one! And relatively unhurt."

Relatively, because her head ached where she had hit it.

Putting that aside, she shoved her car into Reverse, hoping no one had seen what had just transpired. She put her foot down—gently, this time—on the gas, and pressed, but aside from the wheels making an awful whining noise, nothing happened. When she applied more gas, the whining sound increased to a shriek, but the car did not move.

With an edge of franticness, she tried one more time, but her car was stuck fast and refused to budge.

With a sigh of defeat, she turned the car off, rested her aching head against the steering wheel and gave in to the temptation to mull over her bad luck.

No fiancé.

No job.

Those two events linked in a way that had become fodder for the office gossip mill. And possibly beyond. Maybe she was the laughingstock of the entire business community.

At least she still had her charity work. But the sad fact was, though the charity was so worthwhile, it limped along, desperately needing someone prominent—*exactly like Kiernan McAllister*—to thrust it to the next level.

So engrossed was she in her mulling that she shrieked with alarm when her car door was yanked open, spilling cold air into it, stealing the one thing she had been grateful for—warmth—instantly. She reared back from the steering wheel.

"Are you all right?"

The voice was deep and masculine and might have been reassuring. Except for the man it was attached to.

No. No. NO.

This was not how she had intended to meet Kiernan McAllister!

"I seem to be stuck," Stacy said with all the dignity she could muster. After the initial glance, she grasped the steering wheel and looked straight ahead, as if she was planning on going somewhere.

She felt her attempt at dignity might have failed, because he said, his voice the calm, steady voice of someone who had found another standing at the precipice, "That's all right. Let's get you out of there, and see what the damage is."

"Mostly to your garden, I'm afraid."

"I'm not worried about my garden." Again, that calm, talking-her-down-from-the-ledge tone of voice.

"Here. Take my hand."

She needed to reclaim her dignity by insisting she was fine. But when she opened her mouth, not a single sound came out.

"Take my hand."

This time, it was a command more than a request. Weakly, it felt like something of a relief to have choice taken away from her!

As if in a dream, Stacy put her hand in his. She felt it close around hers, warm and strong, and found herself pulled, with seemingly effortless might out of the car and straight into a wall of…man.

She should have felt the cold instantly. Instead, she felt like Charlie Chaplin doing a "slipping on a banana peel" routine. Her legs seemed to be shooting out in different directions.

She yanked free of his hands and threw herself against his chest, hugging tight.

And felt the warmth of it. And the shock. Bare skin? It was snowing out. How was it possible he was bare chested?

Who cares? a little voice whispered in accompaniment to the tingle moving up her spine. Given how humiliating her circumstances, she should not be so aware of the steely firmness of silky flesh and the sensation of being intimately close to pure power. She *really* should not be proclaiming the experience *delicious*.

"Whoa." He unglued her from him and put her slightly away, his hands settled on her shoulders. "Neither you nor your car appear properly shod for this weather."

He was right. Her feet were stylishly clad in a ballet slipper style shoe by a famous designer. She had bought the red slippers—à la Dorothy in the *Wizard of Oz*—when she had been more able to afford such whims.

The shoes had no grip on the sole. Stacy was no better prepared for snow than her car had been, and she was inordinately grateful for his steady-ing hands on her shoulders.

"What have you got on?" he asked, his tone incredulous.

The question really should have been what did he have on—since she was peripherally aware it was not much—but she glanced down at herself, anyway.

The shoes added a light Bohemian touch to an otherwise ultraconservative, just-above-the-knee gray skirt that she had paired with dark tights and a white blouse. At the last moment she had donned a darker gray sweater, which she was glad for now, as the snow fell around her. Noth-ing about her outfit—not even the shoes—com-manded that incredulous tone.

Then, she dared glance fully at her rescuer and realized his question about what she had on was not in the context of her very stylish outfit at all. He was referring to her tires!

"Not even all seasons," he said, squinting past her at the front tire that rested on top of what had been, no doubt, a very expensive shrub. His tone was disapproving. "Summer tires. What were you thinking?"

It was terribly difficult to drag her attention away this unexpectedly delicious encounter with *the* Kiernan McAllister and focus on the question. She felt as if her voice was coming from under water when she answered.

"I've never put winter tires on my car," she confessed. "And if I were going to, it would not occur to me to do it in October. It is the season of falling leaves and pumpkins, not this."

"You could have asked for me to send a car," he said sternly.

Stacy contemplated that. *She* could have asked *the* Kiernan McAllister to send a car? In what universe? Obviously—and sadly—he was expecting someone else.

Or, was there the possibility Caroline had done more than give her an address? Did she have some kind of in with him? Had she set something up for Stacy?

That was her imagination again, because it was not likely he would be so intent on giving an interview he would send a car!

"Were you not prepared at all for mountain driving?"

"Not at all," she admitted. "I was born and

raised in Vancouver. You know how often we get snow there."

At his grunt of what she interpreted as disapproval, she felt compelled to rush on. "Though I've always dreamed of a winter holiday. Skating on a frozen pond, learning to ski. That kind of thing. Now, I'm not so sure about that. Winter seems quite a bit more pleasant in movies and pictures and snow globes. Maybe I should just fast-forward to the hot chocolate in front of the fire."

Was she chattering? Oh, God, she was chattering nervously, and it wasn't just her teeth! *Shut up,* she ordered herself, but she had to add, "Humph. Reality and imagination collide, again."

Story of her life: imagining walking down the aisle, her gorgeous white dress flowing out behind her, toward a man who looked at her with such love and such longing…

She did not want to be having those kinds of treacherous thoughts around *this* man.

"I always liked this reality," McAllister said, and he actually reached out his free hand and caught a snowflake with it. Then he yanked his hand back abruptly, and the line around his mouth tightened and Stacy saw something mercurial in his storm-gray eyes.

She realized he had recalled, after the words came out of his mouth, that it was this reality—in the form of an avalanche—that had caused the death of his brother-in-law.

Sympathy clawed at her throat, as did a sense of knowing he was holding something inside that was eating him like acid.

It was a lot to understand from a glimpse of something in his eyes, from the way his mouth had changed, but this was exactly what Caroline had meant about Stacy's ability to get to the heart of a story.

For some reason—probably from the loss of her family when she was a child—she had a superhoned sense of intuition that had left her with an ability to see people with extraordinary clarity and tell their stories deeply and profoundly.

Not that McAllister looked as if he would be willing to have his story told at all, his secrets revealed, his feelings probed.

Stacy had a sudden sense if she did get to the heart of this man, as Caroline had wistfully suggested, she would find it broken.

McAllister's face was closed now, as if he sensed he had let his guard down just for that instant and that it might have revealed too much to her.

"What did you do when you lost control?" he asked her.

Of her life? How on earth could he tell? Was he has intuitive as she herself was?

But, to her relief, his attention was focused, disapprovingly, on her tires. He was still keeping her upright on the slippery ground, his hand now firmly clamped on her elbow, but if he was feeling the same sensation of being singed that she was, it in no way showed in his face. He had the look of a man who was always composed and in control.

"What did I do? I closed my eyes, and held on for dear life, of course!"

"Imagining a good outcome?" he said drily.

She nodded sadly. The collision with reality was more than evident.

He sighed, with seeming long-suffering, though their acquaintance had been extremely brief!

"You might want to keep in mind, for next

time, if you lose control on ice, to try and steer into the spin, rather than away from it."

"That doesn't seem right."

"I know, it goes against everyone's first instinct. But really, that's what you do. You go with it, instead of fighting it."

The sense of being singed increased when Stacy became suddenly and intensely aware that, despite the snow falling in large and chilly flakes all around them, despite the fact the driveway was pure ice, the question really should not have been what she had on for tires—or for clothes! That should not have been the question at all, given what he had on.

Which was next to nothing!

Maybe she had hit her head harder than she thought, and this whole thing was a dream. The scene was surreal after all.

How could it be possible McAllister was out here in his driveway, one hand gripping her firmly, glaring at her tires, when he was dressed in nothing more than a pair of shove-on sandals, a towel cinched around his waist?

The shock of it made her release the arm she clutched, and the wisps of her remaining sympathy were blown away as if before a strong wind. All that remained was awareness of him in a very different way.

She would have staggered back—and probably slipped again—but when she had let go, he had continued to hold on.

His warmth and his strength were like electricity, but not the benign kind that powered the toaster.

No, the furious, unpredictable kind. The lightning-bolt-that-could-tear-open-the-sky kind. The kind that could split apart trees and turn the world to fire.

Stacy realized the hammering of her heart during the slippery trip into the mountains, and after she had bounced over the curb into the fountain, had been but a pale prelude to the speeds her heart could attain!

CHAPTER TWO

KIERNAN MCALLISTER WATCHED the pulse in the woman's throat. The accident had obviously affected her more than she wanted to let on. Her face was very pale and he considered the awful possibility she was going to keel over, either because she was close to fainting or because her shoes were so unsuited to this kind of ground.

As he watched, her hand, tiny and pale, fluttered to her own throat to keep tabs on the wildly beating tattoo of her pulse, and McAllister tightened his grip on her even more.

"Are you okay?" he asked again. He could feel his brow furrow as he looked in her face.

He had told his sister, Adele, not to send assistance. He had told her, in no uncertain terms, that he found it insulting that she thought he needed it. She seemed to have agreed, but he should have guessed she only pretended to acquiesce.

"I think I'm just shaken."

The girl—no, she wasn't a girl, despite her diminutive size—had a voice that was low and husky, a lovely softness to it, unconsciously sexy. She was, in fact, a lovely young woman. Dark curls sprang untamed around a delicate, pale, elfin face. Her eyes were green and huge, her nose a little button, her chin had a certain defiant set to it.

Kiernan's annoyance at his sister grew.

If she had needed to send someone—and in her mind, apparently she had—he would have hoped for someone no-nonsense and practical. Someone who arrived in a car completely outfitted for winter and in sturdy shoes. In other words someone who coped, pragmatically, as a matter of course, with every eventuality. If he was going to picture that someone he would picture someone middle-aged, dowdy and stern enough to intimidate Ivan the Terrible into instant submission.

Now, he felt as if he had two people, other than himself, to be responsible for!

"You're sure you are all right?" He cast a glance at her car. Maybe he could get it unstuck and convince her to disobey his sister's orders, whatever they were, and leave him alone here.

Alone. That was what called to him these days, the seduction of silence, of not being around people. The cabin was perfect. Hard to access, no cell service, spotty internet.

His sister didn't see his quest for solitude as a good thing. "You just go up there and mull over things that can't be changed!" his sister had accused him.

And perhaps that was true. Certainly, the presence of his little nephew did not leave much time for mulling! And perhaps that had been Adele's plan. His sister could be diabolical after all.

But the woman who had just arrived looked more like distraction than heaven-sent helper, so he was going to figure out how to get her unstuck and set her on her way no matter what Adele had to say about it.

For some reason, he did not want the curly-headed, green-eyed, red-shoed woman to make it past the first guard and into his house!

He regarded her thoughtfully, trying to figure out why he felt he did not want to let her in. And then he knew. Despite the fact the accident had left her shaken, she seemed determined to not let it affect her.

Look at the shoes! She was one of those positive, sunny, impractical people and he did not want her invading his space.

When had he come to like the dark of his own misery and loneliness so much?

"Yes, I'm fine," she said, her voice, tremulous with bravery, piercing the darkness of his own thoughts. "More embarrassed than anything."

"And well you should be." The faint sympathy he had felt for her melted. "A person with a grain of sense and so little winter driving experience should not have tackled these roads today. I told her not to send you."

She blinked at that. Opened her mouth, then closed it, looked down at her little red shoes and ineffectually tried to scrape the snow off them.

"I detest stubborn women," he muttered. "Why would you travel today?"

"Perhaps it wasn't my most sensible decision," she said, and he watched the chin that had hinted at a stubborn nature tilt upward a touch, "but I can't guarantee the result would not have been similar, even on the finest summer day."

He lifted an eyebrow at her, intrigued despite himself.

"My second name is Murphy, for my maternal grandfather, and it is very suiting. I am like a poster child for Murphy's Law."

He had the feeling she was trying to keep things light in the face of the deliberate dark judgment in his own features, so he did not respond to the lightness of her tone, just raised his eyebrow even higher at her.

"Murphy's Law?"

"You know," she clarified, trying for a careless grin and missing by a mile. "Anything that can go wrong, will."

He stared at her. For a moment, the crystal clear green of those eyes clouded, and he felt some thread of shared experience, of unspeakable sorrow, trying to bind them together.

His sense of needing to get rid of her strengthened. But then he saw the blood in her hair.

Stacy could have kicked herself! What on earth had made her say that to him? It was not at all in keeping with the new her: strong, composed, sophisticated. You didn't blurt out things like that to a perfect stranger! She had intended it to sound light; instead, it sounded like a pathetic play for sympathy!

And, damn it, sometimes when you opened that door you did not know what was going to come through.

And what came through for her was a powerful vision of the worst moment of *anything that can go wrong will* in her entire life. She was standing outside her high school gym. She closed her eyes against it, but it came anyway.

Standing outside the high school waiting anxiously, just wanting to be anywhere but there. Waiting for the car that never came. A teacher finding her long after everyone else had gone home, wrapping her in her own sweater, because Stacy was shivering. She already knew there was only one reason that her father would not have come. Her whole world gone so terribly and completely wrong in an instant...left craving the one thing she could never have again.

Her family.

She had hit her head harder than she thought! That's what was causing this. Or was it the look she had glimpsed ever so briefly in his own eyes?

The look that had given her the sensation that he was a man bereft?

"You actually don't look okay," he decided.

She opened her eyes to see him studying her too intently. Just what every woman—even one newly devoted to independence—wanted to hear from Kiernan McAllister!

"I don't?"

"You're not going to faint, are you?"

"No!" Her denial was vehement, given the fact that she had been contemplating that very possibility—heart implosion—only seconds ago.

"You've gone quite pale." He was looking at her too intensely.

"It's my coloring," she said. "I always look pale."

This was, unfortunately, more than true. Though she had the dark brown hair of her father, she had not inherited his olive complexion. Her mother had been a redhead, and she had her ultrapale, sensitive skin and green eyes.

"You are an unusual combination of light and dark." She squirmed under his gaze, until he tightened his hold.

"Remember Murphy's Law," he warned her. "It's very slippery out here, and those shoes look more suited to a bowling alley than a fresh snowfall."

A bowling alley? "They're Kleinbacks," she insisted on informing him, trying to shore up her quickly disintegrating self-esteem. The shoes, after all proclaimed *arrival,* not disaster.

"Well, you'll be lyin'-on-your-backs if you aren't careful in them. You don't want to add to your injuries."

"Injuries?"

Still holding her one arm firmly, he used his other—he seemed to have his cell phone in it— and whipped off the towel he had around his waist!

Still juggling the towel and the phone, he found a dry corner of it, and pressed it, with amazing gentleness, onto the top of her head. "I didn't see it at first, amongst the chocolate curls—"

Chocolate curls? It was the nicest way her hair had ever been described! Did that mean he was noticing more about her than his sack-of-potatoes hold had indicated?

"—but there's blood in your hair."

His voice was perfection, a silk scarf caressing the sensitive area of her neck.

"There is?" She peeked at him around the edges of the towel.

He dabbed at her hair—again, she was taken with the tenderness of his touch, when he radiated such a powerful aura—and then he turned the towel to her, proof.

It looked like an extremely expensive towel, brilliant white, probably Egyptian cotton, and now it had little speckles of red from her blood. Though for some reason, maybe the knock on the head, the sight of all that blood was not nearly as alarming to her as he was.

Since he had removed the towel, Stacy forced herself not to let her gaze stray from his face. Water was sliding out of the dark silk of his hair and down the utterly and devastatingly attractive lines of his features.

"You aren't naked, are you?" she asked, her voice a squeak of pure dismay.

Something twitched around the sensual line of his mouth as McAllister contemplated Stacy's question, but she couldn't really tell if he was amused or annoyed by it.

His mouth opened, then closed, and then, his

eyes never leaving her face, he said evenly, "No, I'm not."

She dared to unglue her eyes from his face. They skittered over the very naked line of his broad shoulders, down the beautiful cut of chest muscles made more beautiful by the snowflakes that melted on them and sent beads of waters sliding down to the ridged muscle of washboard abs. Riding low on his hips…her eyes flew back to the relative safety of his face.

Only that wasn't really safe, either.

"Underwear?" she squeaked.

He regarded her thoughtfully for a moment. She resisted an urge to squirm, again, under the firm hands at her elbow, and his stripping gaze.

"Kleinbacks," he said, straight-faced.

She was pretty sure the designer company did not make men's underwear, and that was confirmed when something very like a smile, however reluctant, played along the hard line of those lips. Stunned, Stacy realized she was being *teased* by Kiernan McAllister.

But the light that appeared for a moment in his eyes was gone almost instantly, making her aware he had caught himself lightening up, and not liked it. Not liked it one little bit.

"Swim trunks." His voice was gravelly, amusement stripped from it.

"Oh!" She sagged with relief, then looked, just to make sure. They were really very nice swim trunks, not the scanty kind that triathletes wore. Still, there was quite a bit more of him uncovered than covered, and she felt herself turn scarlet as she watched a another snow drop melt and slide past the taut muscles of his stomach and into the waistband of his shorts.

"It doesn't really seem like swimming weather," she offered, her voice strangled.

"I was in the hot tub in the back of the house when I heard the commotion out here."

"Oh! Of course." She tried to sound as if she was well acquainted with the kind of people who spent snowy afternoons doing business from their hot tubs—he did have his phone with him, after all—but she was fairly certain she did not pull it off.

Knowing what she did about him, it occurred to her that perhaps, despite the presence of the phone, he wasn't doing business. One thing she knew from her life interviewing high-powered execs? They were attached to those phones as though they were lifelines!

Kiernan McAllister might be entertaining someone in his hot tub.

"Alone," he said, as if he had read her thoughts.

She didn't like the idea that he might be able to read her thoughts. But there was also something about the way he said *alone* that made her think of icy, windswept mountain peaks and a soul gone cold.

Even though he was the one with no clothes on, in the middle of a snowstorm, it was Stacy who shivered. She tried to tell herself it was from snow melting off her neck and slithering down her back, but she knew that was not the entire truth.

It was pure awareness of the man who stood before her, his complexities both unsettling her and reluctantly intriguing her. His hands resting, warm and strong—dare she consider the thought, protectively—on her. How on earth could he be so completely unselfconscious? And why wasn't he trembling with cold?

Obviously, his skin was heated from the hot

tub, not that he was the kind of man who trembled! He was supremely comfortable with himself, radiating a kind of confidence that could not be manufactured.

Plus, Stacy's mind filled in helpfully, he had quite a reputation. He would not be unaccustomed to being in some state of undress in front of a lady.

Impossibly, she could feel her cheeks turning even more crimson, and he showed no inclination to put her out of her misery. He regarding her appraisingly, snow melting on his heated skin, a cloud of steam rising around him.

Finally, he seemed to realize it was very cold out here!

"Let's get in," he suggested. She heard reluctance in his voice. He did not want her in his house!

She was not sure why, though it didn't seem unreasonable. A stranger plows into your fountain. You hardly want to entertain them.

But he was expecting someone. He didn't want to entertain that person, either?

"I'll take a closer look at your head. There's not

a whole lot of blood, I'm almost certain it's superficial. We'll get you into Whistler if it's not."

It occurred to her he was a man who would do the right thing even if it was not what he particularly wanted to do.

And that he would not like people who did the wrong thing. She shivered at the thought. He misinterpreted the shiver as cold and strengthened his grip on her, as if he didn't trust her not to keel over or slip badly on his driveway. He turned her away from her car and toward the warmth of his house.

Aside from her car in the garden, the driveway was empty. The household vehicles were no doubt parked in the five-car garage off to one side.

The house inspired awe. If this was a cottage, what on earth did McAllister's main residence look like?

The house was timber framed, the lower portions of it faced in river rock. Gorgeous, golden logs, so large three people holding hands would barely form a circle around them, acted as pillars for the front entryway. The entry doors were hand carved and massive, the windows huge, plentiful and French-paned, the rooflines sweeping and complicated.

Through the softly falling flakes of snow, Stacy was certain she felt exactly how Cinderella must have felt the first time she saw the castle.

Or maybe, she thought, with a small shiver of pure apprehension, more like Beauty when she found Beast's lair.

McAllister let go of her finally when he reached the front door and held it open for her. She was annoyed with herself that she missed the security of his touch instantly, and yet the house seemed to embrace her. The rush of warm air that greeted her was lovely, the house even lovelier.

Stacy's breath caught in her throat as she gaped at her surroundings.

"It's beautiful," she breathed. "Like upscale hunting lodge—very upscale—meets five-star hotel."

"It suits me," he said, and then as an afterthought, "far more than my condo in Vancouver."

Again, her intuition kicked in, and this time the reporter in her went on red alert. Was that a clue that he was going to leave his high-powered life behind him as rumors had been saying for months?

McAllister turned, stepped out of his sandals, expecting her to follow him. Stacy realized she couldn't tromp through the house in her now very wet—and probably ruined—shoes. She scraped them off her feet, dropped her wet sweater beside them, and then she was left scrambling to catch up to his long strides, as it had never even occurred to him that she was not on his heels.

As McAllister led her through his magnificent home, Stacy was further distracted from the confession she should have been formulating about why she was really here, by not just the long length of his naked back but the unexpected beauty of his space and what it said about him.

The design style was breathtaking. Old blended with new seamlessly. Modern met antique. Rustic lines met sleek clean ones and merged.

There were hand-knotted Turkish rugs and bearskins, side by side, modern art and Western paintings, deer antler light fixtures and ones that looked to be by the famous crystal maker, Swarovski. There were ancient woven baskets beside contemporary vases.

The decor style was rugged meets sophisticated, and Stacy thought it reflected the man with startling accuracy.

"I've never seen floors like this," she murmured.

"Tigerwood. It actually gets richer as it ages."

"Like people," she said softly.

"If they invest properly," he agreed.

"That is not what I meant!"

He cast a look over his shoulder at her, and she saw he looked irritated.

"People," she said firmly, "become richer because they accumulate wisdom and life experience."

He snorted derisively. "Or," he countered, "they become harder. This floor is a hundred and seventy percent harder than oak. I chose it because I wanted something hard."

And she could see that that was also what he wanted for himself: a hard, impenetrable surface.

"This floor will last forever," he said with satisfaction.

"Unlike people?" she challenged him.

"You said it, I didn't." She heard the cynicism and yet contemplated his desire for something lasting. He was an avowed bachelor and had been even before the accident. But had the death of his brother-in-law made him even more cynical about what lasted and what didn't?

Clearly, it had.

They walked across exotic hardwood floors into a great room. The walls soared upward, at least sixteen feet high, the ceilings held up by massive timbers. A fireplace, floor to ceiling, constructed of the same river rock that was on the exterior of the house, anchored one end of the room.

A huge television was mounted above a solid old barn beam mantel. It was on, with no sound. A football game in process. A wall of glass—the kind that folded back in the summer to make indoor and outdoor space blend perfectly—led out to a vast redwood deck.

Through falling snow, Stacy could see a deep and quiet forest beyond the deck and past that, the silent, jagged walls of the mountains.

To one side of that deck, where it did not impede the sweeping views from the great room, steam escaped from the large hot tub that her arrival had pulled McAllister from.

The tub seemed as if it were made for entertaining large groups of people of the kind she had written about in her former life. She had never attended a gathering worthy of this kind of space. Or been invited to one, either. As reporter, she had been on the outside of that lifestyle looking in.

The room made Stacy uncomfortably and awkwardly aware she was way out of her league here.

What league? she asked herself, annoyed. She wasn't here to marry the man! She just wanted to talk to him.

Besides, it seemed to her that a room like this cried for that thing called family. In fact, she could feel an ache in the back of her throat as she thought of that.

"Are you coming?"

She realized she had stopped and he had kept going. Now he glanced back at her, and she sensed his impatience. She was trying to savor this unexpected glimpse into a different world, and he wanted their enforced time together over!

Given that, it would be foolish to ask him the question that had popped into her mind the moment she had entered the grandeur of this room. But ask she did!

"Do you spend Christmas here?" She could hear the wistfulness in her own voice.

He stopped, those formidable brows lowered. "I don't particularly like Christmas."

"You don't like Christmas?"

"No." He had folded his arms across his chest, and his look did not invite any more questions.

But she could not help herself! "Is it recent? Your aversion to Christmas?" she asked, wondering if his antipathy had something to do with the death of his brother-in-law. From experience, she knew that, after a loss, special occasions could be unbearably hard.

"No," he said flatly. "I have always hated Christmas."

His look was warning her not to pursue it but for a reason she couldn't quite fathom—maybe because this beautiful house begged for a beautiful Christmas, she did not leave it.

"A tree would look phenomenal over there," she said stubbornly.

His eyes narrowed on her. She was pretty sure

he was not accustomed to people offering him an opinion he had not asked for!

"We—" He paused at the *we,* and she saw that look in his eyes. Then, he seemed to force himself to go on, his tone stripped of emotion. "We always go away at Christmas, preferably someplace warm. We've never spent Christmas in this house."

Her disappointment felt sharp. She ordered herself to silence, but her voice mutinied. "It's never had a Christmas tree?"

He folded his arms more firmly over his chest, his body language clearly saying *unmovable.* She repeated the order for silence, but she could not seem to stop her voice.

"Think of the size of tree you could put there! And there's room for kids to ride trikes across the floors, and grandparents to sit by the fire."

He looked extremely annoyed.

She could picture it all. Generations of family sitting in the two huge distressed leather sofas faced each other over a priceless rug, teenagers running in wet from the hot tub, eggnog on the coffee table made out of burled wood. Toys littering the floor.

Over there, in that open-concept kitchen with its industrial-sized stainless-steel fridge, the massive granite-topped island could be full of snacks, the espresso machine pumping out coffee, or maybe you could make hot chocolate in them, she wasn't certain.

"I guess in your line of work," he said gruffly, "you're allowed a certain amount of magical thinking."

What kind of work did he think she did? And why couldn't she just leave it at that?

"It's not magical," she said through clenched teeth. "It's real. It can be real."

He looked annoyed and unconvinced.

Why had she started this? She could feel something like tears stinging the back of her eyes.

"You have that about-to-faint look again," he said, coming back to her. "I think you hit your head harder than we realize."

"I think you're right," she said. She ordered herself to stop speaking. But she didn't.

CHAPTER THREE

"IF I HAD a room like this? That is what I would want to fill it with," the woman said. "The important things. The things that really last. The things that are real. Love. Family."

Real. Kiernan could tell her a thing or two about the reality of love and family that would wipe that dreamy look off her face. But why? Let her have her illusions.

They were no threat to him.

Or maybe they were, because just for a flicker of a moment he felt a whisper of longing sneak along his spine.

He shook it off. He just wanted to have a look at the bump on her head and send her on her way. He did not want to hear about her sugarplum visions of a wonderful world!

"Nothing lasts," he told her, his voice a growl.

Stacy went very still. For a moment she looked as if she might argue, but then his words seemed to hit her, like arrows let loose that had found her heart.

To his dismay, for a moment he glimpsed in her face a sorrow he thought matched his own. He was intrigued but had enough good sense not to follow up! Not to encourage her in any way to share her vision with him.

"Follow me," he said. "I think I've got a first-aid kit in my bathroom."

His bathroom? Didn't he have a first-aid kit somewhere else? He did, but it was outside and around the back of the house, where the staging area for outdoor excursions was, where he stored the outdoor equipment.

No, it was sensible to take her to the closest first-aid kit, to keep her out of the cold, to not take her through more snow in those ridiculous shoes.

But through his bedroom? Into his bathroom? It occurred to him that he should have sat her down in the kitchen and brought the first-aid kit to her.

He was not thinking with his normal razor-sharp processes, which was understandable. He told himself it had nothing to do with the unexpected arrival of a beautiful woman in his fountain and everything to do with Ivan.

He hesitated at the double doors to his master suite and then flung them open and watched her closely as she preceded him. He saw the room through her eyes, which were wide and awed.

The ceiling soared upward, magnificent and timber framed. But here the floors, instead of being hardwood, were carpeted with a thick, plush pile that their feet sank into. There was a huge bed, the bedding and the abundance of pillows in a dozen shades of gray.

She was blushing as she looked at the bed, which he should have found amusing as all getout. Instead, he found it reluctantly endearing.

Who blushed anymore?

Something that heightened color in her cheeks, the way she caught her plump lower lip between her teeth, made Kiernan's mouth go dry, and so he led her hastily through to the bathroom. Again, he saw it through her eyes. A wall of windows opened to the deck and hot tub area.

There was a shower a dozen people could have gotten into, and her blush deepened when she looked at that.

He'd never shared this room with anyone, but let her think what she wanted. It might keep him safe from this niggling awareness of her that was bugging him the way a single gnat could spoil a perfect summer day on the hammock with a book.

She stared at the deep, stand-alone tub and swallowed hard. While the shower might hold dozens, it was more than evident the tub could only comfortably fit two! Her eyes flitted wildly around the room and then stopped and widened.

Her eyes, he noticed, annoyed with himself, were green as the moss that clung to the stones of the hot spring deep in the mountains behind this cottage.

"That is not a fireplace," she whispered. "In your bathroom?"

"You want it on?" he asked innocently. "Are you cold?"

He was fairly sure it was evident to even her, with her aura of innocence, that a fireplace like that was not about cold but about romance.

And yet he did not like thinking about her in that light. It was evident to him, on a very brief acquaintance, she was not the type of woman who would share his vision of romance.

For him, it was a means to an end, the age-old game of seduction.

The remarks about his floors and the suitability of his room for a Christmas tree were little hints she was not his type. By her own admission, she was the kind of girl who believed in love and things lasting.

Romancing a girl like her would be hard work! He was willing to bet, despite her awe of the room, it would require something a little less superficial than a bathtub and a fireplace. Romancing a girl like her would require time and patience and a willingness to be a better person.

No, he would stick with his type. Because his type required nothing of him but a few baubles and some good times, no real emotional engagement.

He had always been like that, avoiding emotional attachment. He had been like that before his friend Danner had died. Kiernan had a sudden unwelcome memory of Christmas ornaments being smashed. He suspected the memory had erupted out of nowhere because

Murphy here had seen Christmas in a room where it had never been. Kiernan's early life had always been threaded through with the tension of unpredictability, Christmas worse than most times of year.

For a while, having survived the minefield of his childhood, Kiernan had enjoyed the illusion of complete control. He had a sense of making not just his world safe and predictable, but that of his sister, Adele, too.

Yup, he had felt like quite the hero. And then Danner had died. Plunging him into a dark place where his real power in the world seemed horribly limited, where hope and dreams seemed like the most dangerous of things.

And none of that fit with a girl like this, who, whether she knew it or not, wore dreams on her sleeves. Who, despite—if her eyes were any indicator—having gone a round or two with life, seemed to still have that inexplicable ability to believe…

"Sure," she said after a moment, startling him out of his thoughts. "Put it on. The fireplace." She giggled. "I may never pass this way again."

"We can only hope," he muttered, and saw her

flinch, the smile die, the words striking her like arrows again.

Just a reminder of how she was soft and he was hard, a reason this was never going anywhere, except him standing on the stairs seeing her off as she drove away.

"Nothing personal," he said. "It just wasn't my idea for you to come. I don't need you."

Having done quite enough damage—he really should not be allowed around these sensitive types—Kiernan turned from her and flicked a switch so that the flames within the fireplace licked to life.

"I've changed my mind," she said proudly. "I don't care to have it on."

See? In very short time his abrasive self was managing to hurt her. Not making any effort to hide his impatience, Kiernan flicked the fire back off and gestured at an upholstered chaise.

Once she was settled, he came back, towered over her and studied the top of her head. "I'm just going to clean it first. We'll see what we've got. Ironic, isn't it, that I'm rescuing you?"

"In what way?" she stammered.

"You're supposed to be rescuing me."

* * *

Stacy studied Kiernan and realized his tone was deeply sardonic. Despite the glimpses of shadows she had detected in his eyes, she was not sure she had ever seen a man who looked less like he would appreciate rescuing than Kiernan McAllister!

He was bigger in real life than photos had prepared her for, the breadth of his shoulders blocking out the view of the fireplace!

The bathroom was huge, but with him leaning over her, his real-life stature left her feeling shocked. Even though Kiernan McAllister had graced the covers of zillions of magazines, including, eight times, the one she no longer worked for, nothing could have prepared her for him in this kind of proximity.

Pictures, of course, did not have a scent clinging to them. His filled her nostrils: it was as if he had come, not from a hot tub, but from the forest around this amazing house. McAllister smelled richly of pine, as if he had absorbed the essence of the snow-laden trees through his pores!

He was considered not only Vancouver's most successful businessman, but also its most eligible bachelor, and here in the bathroom with him, his scent filling her senses, his hands gentle on her injured head, it was easy to see why!

In each of those photos that Stacy had seen of him, McAllister was breathtakingly handsome and sure of himself. Behind that engaging smile, he had oozed the confidence and self-assurance of the very successful and very wealthy. His grooming had always been perfect: smooth shaven, every dark hair in place, his custom-made clothing hinting at but not showing a perfect male body.

In those pictures, he looked like a man who could handle anything the world tossed at him, smile and toss it right back.

And that's what he had a track record for doing. From daring real estate deals to providing start-up funds for fledgling companies that no one else would take a risk on, McAllister had developed a reputation as being tough, fair and savvy. In the business world, his instincts were considered brilliant.

Not to mention that, with his amazing looks, McAllister was that most eligible bachelor that every unmarried woman dreamed—secretly or openly—of landing.

And McAllister had availed himself to every perk his considerable fortune allowed him. He had squired some of the most beautiful and famous women in the world on that arm that Stacy had just touched.

But, despite having it all, he seemed driven to more, and he had as casually sought danger as some men would sample a fine wine.

And it was that penchant for the adrenaline rush that had led from *that* McAllister to this one.

Being able to watch him while he tended her head, she could see his silver-gray eyes were mesmerizing and yet different in some fundamental way from how he appeared in pictures.

Her mind grappled to figure out what that difference was, but the distraction of his near nakedness, the luxury of the bathroom and his hands on her head were proving formidable.

"Ouch."

"Sorry."

She deliberately looked at the floor instead of up into his face to break the trance she was in. Instead, it felt oddly intimate and totally inappropriate that Stacy could see the naked length of his lower legs. His feet were totally bare.

And, she thought, entirely sexy.

But she didn't find feet sexy. Did she?

Since his feet provided no more reprieve from the terrible war of sensation going on within her, Stacy dragged her gaze away from his toes and back up the length of him. Despite his disheveled appearance—his hair, always perfectly groomed for magazine shoots, was sticking up in a cowlick at the back of his head, and his cheeks and the jut of that formidable chin were shadowed in dark whiskers—when Stacy looked into his face, she had to swallow a gulp of pure intimidation.

Kiernan McAllister radiated a kind of power that could not be tarnished by arriving at the scene of an accident, dripping wet and with a towel around his waist. Even though her job at *Icons of Business* had entailed interviewing dozens of very successful businesspeople, Stacy was not sure she had ever encountered such a prime example of pure of *presence* before.

McAllister's wet hair, the color of just-brewed coffee, was curling at the tips. The stubble on his face accentuated the hard, masculine lines of his features.

The out-of-the-storm look of his hair and being unshaven gave him a distinctly roguish look, and despite his state of undress, he could have been a pirate relishing his next conquest, like a high-wayman about to draw his sword.

His eyes were a shade of silver that added to her sense that he could be dangerous in the most tantalizing of ways.

In the pictures she had seen of him, his eyes had intrigued, a faint light at the back of them that she had interpreted as mischievous, as if all his incredible successes in the business world were nothing more than a big game and it was a game that he was winning.

But, of course, that was before the accident where his brother-in-law had been killed.

There was the difference. Now McAllister's eyes had something in them as shattered as glass, cool, a barrier that he did not want penetrated.

By someone looking for a story. In that moment, Stacy knew Caroline had not set up anything for her. And she also knew, without asking, he would turn her down flat if she requested an interview.

He stepped back from her, regarded his handiwork on her head. "I think we're done here," he said, evidently pleased with his first-aid skills.

He once again offered his hand. She took it and he pulled her from the chair. She relished the feeling of his hand, but he let her go as soon as she was standing. She faced herself in the mirror. It was much worse than she thought.

The top of her hair was almost completely covered with a tightly taped down piece of gauze.

Now she really did look and feel like the poster child for Murphy's Law. Everything that could go wrong, *had*. Who wanted to look like this in the presence of such a devastatingly attractive man?

Even if he was sardonic. And didn't believe in Christmas. Or love.

"That's going to be murder to get off," she said, when she saw he had caught her dismayed expression.

"Isn't it?" he said, apparently pleased that his handiwork was going to be so hard to remove.

She sighed. It was definitely time to set him

straight about who she really was and what she wanted. She took a deep breath.

The phone that he had set on the counter began to ring.

Only it was the oddest ring she had ever heard. It sounded exactly like a baby squawking! There was no way a man like McAllister picked a ringtone like that!

In a split second, Kiernan McAllister went from looking relaxed and at ease with himself to a warrior ready to do battle! Stacy watched his face grow cold, remote, underscoring that sense of a solider being ready for whatever came next.

"What on earth?" she whispered, taking in his stance and his hardened facial features. "What's the matter?"

"It's time," he said, his tone terse. "He's awake."

"Who's awake?"

McAllister said nothing, his gaze on the phone, his brow furrowed in consternation. If he were a general, she had the feeling he would be checking his weapons, strapping on his armor, calling out his instructions to his soldiers.

"That isn't a cell phone, is it?" Stacy asked slowly. McAllister was staring at it as if he was a tourist in some exotic place who had discovered a snake under his bed.

The squawking sound escalated, and McAllister took a deep breath, squared his shoulders.

"A phone?" he asked, his voice impatient. "What kind of person has a phone in the hot tub?"

In her career she had met dozens of men who she did not doubt took their phones everywhere with them, including into their hot tubs! Now, she could see clearly he would not be one of them.

"Cell phones don't work up here. The mountains block the signal. I think it's part of what I like about the place." He frowned as if realizing he had told her something about himself he didn't want to.

That he needed a break from the demands of his business. He was no doubt the kind of driven individual who would see some kind of failure in that.

But before she could contemplate that too long, the phone made that squawking sound again, louder.

"What is it then, if it's not your phone?"

"It's the monitor," he said.

"The monitor," she repeated.

"The baby monitor," he said, as if she had not already guessed it.

She stared at it with him, listened to the squawking noises emitting from it. The monitor was small and state-of-the-art, it looked almost exactly like a cell phone.

But if was definitely a monitor, and there was definitely a baby on the other end of it!

CHAPTER FOUR

BABY?

Stacy prided herself on the fact that she had arrived prepared! She knew everything there was to know about Kiernan McAllister.

And he did not have a baby!

McAllister folded his arms across the breadth of his naked chest and raised that dark slash of an eyebrow at her. "I told you, you were rescuing me, not the other way around."

"Excuse me?" Stacy said, dazed by this turn of events.

"Your turn to ride to the rescue, though I must say, you haven't exactly inspired confidence so far." He reached out and turned down the volume on the monitor, inspecting her anew, like a general might inspect a newly enlisted person before sending them into battle.

His voice was hard-edged, and faintly amused as he regarded her, and she was struck again that, despite his words, he was the man least likely to need a rescue of any sort. Even if he did need one, he would never ask for it!

"I'm riding to your rescue?" Stacy asked, just to clarify.

It was a good thing he seemed to be being sarcastic, because it would be terrible to break it to him that she was the least likely person to count on for a rescue, her own life being ample evidence of that.

"Just like the cavalry," he said, and cocked his head at her blank expression. "I'm stranded. The fort is under full attack. I have no bullets left. And in rides the cavalry."

"Me?" she squeaked. "I'm the cavalry?"

He eyed her with doubt that appeared to mirror her own, then sighed again. "You are the nanny Adele insisted on sending, aren't you?"

The nanny!

Stacy realized Caroline had not called and set something up for her. Far from it! *A nanny. Kiernan McAllister was expecting a nanny!* That's who he would have sent a car through the snowy day for!

Fortunately, Stacy was saved from having to

answer because he turned and held open the door of the bathroom for her.

"That way," he said. "To the guest room. You can help me temporarily, until I get your car looked after."

In a daze, she turned left and went down the hall ahead of McAllister.

His voice followed her, his tone mulling. "I thought he would sleep longer. He has barely slept since he got here. Who would have thought that one small baby could be so demanding? He doesn't sleep. And he doesn't want to eat. You know what he does?"

Again, he didn't wait for an answer.

"He cries." His voice was lowered, and she thought she detected the slightest admission he might be in over his head. "Not that I couldn't handle it. But, if my sister thinks I need saving, who am I to argue?"

Stacy swallowed hard. What was it about the thought of saving a man like him that made her go almost weak with wanting? But, despite what his sister thought, the look on his face made it very apparent he did not agree!

That was the *old* her that would have liked

him to *need* her, Stacy reminded herself sternly. The old her: naive and romantic, believing in the power of love and hoping for a family gathered in a big room around a Christmas tree.

Obviously, McAllister did not need saving. She had rarely seen a man so self-assured! What man could stand outside dripping wet and barely clothed and act as if nothing was out of the ordinary?

Still, there was that look in his eyes…defiant, daring her to see need in him! Foolishly it made her want to turn toward him, run her hand over the coarse stubble of that jaw and assure him that, yes, she was there to rescue him and that everything would be all right.

Instead, she kept moving forward until she came to an open door and peered inside. There was a playpen set up in the room, and in it was a nest of messy blankets and stuffed toys.

Holding himself up on the bumper, howling with indignation and jumping up and down, was the most beautiful baby she had ever seen. He looked like he was a little over a year, chubby, dark hair every which way, completely adorable in pale blue sleepers that had the snaps done up crooked.

Was he McAllister's baby? While a secret baby would have been the story of the century, her thoughts drifted way too quickly from story potential to far more treacherous territory.

What on earth was Kiernan McAllister doing with a baby when that was what she had always wanted?

It caught her off guard and left her reeling even more than spinning her car into his front garden had!

We want such different things, her ex-boyfriend, Dylan, had said with a sad shake of his head, dismissing her dreams of reclaiming a traditional life like the one she had grown up in as a life sentence of dullness.

Their last night together, the extravagant dinner had made Stacey think he was going to offer her an engagement ring.

Instead, she had been devastated by his invitation to move in with him!

Really, his defection had been the last straw in a life where love had ripped her wide open once too often. To add to the sting of it all, they had

worked in the same office, he her direct supe-
rior, and she had been let go after their breakup,
which she—and everyone else at the office—
knew was entirely unfair.

Still, in the wake of her life disasters, Stacy
had made up her mind she would be wounded by
love and life no more! But now the yearning inside her caused by seeing that Christmas-perfect
great room, and now by thinking of this man before her with a baby, only made her realize how
much work she had yet to do!

Though why, when she knew how much work
she had to do, her eyes would go to McAllister's
lips, she could not be certain. McAllister's lips
were full and bold, the lower one in particular
spine-tinglingly sensual.

Dangerous, she told herself. He was a dangerous kind of man. His lips should be declared the
pillars of salt one should never look at for danger
of being lost forever. She was stunned by both
the peril and intensity of her thoughts.

She was not, after all, who he was expecting,
and she was certainly not a qualified nanny.

But she felt as if she *had* to know the story of
the baby.

And McAllister—despite the outward appearance of confidence—was obviously desperate for help in this particular situation.

And if she could give him that even temporarily, McAllister might be much more amenable to the real reason she had come!

Gratitude could go a long way, after all.

The baby was startled into silence by her appearance. He regarded her with deep suspicion.

As if he knew she was trying to pass herself off as something she was not.

He seemed to make up his mind about her and began to whimper again.

"Ivan, stop it!" McAllister ordered.

The baby, surprisingly, complied.

"Ivan," she said, and walked over to the baby. "Hello, Ivan."

The baby appeared to reconsider his initial assessment of her. He smiled tentatively and made a little gargling noise in his throat. Her heart was lost instantly and completely.

"You don't know my nephew's name?" McAllister asked, startled. "It's Max."

She glanced back at McAllister. His arms were folded over his chest, and he was regarding her with suspicion identical to the baby's seconds earlier.

His nephew. The blanks were filling in, but all the same it was unraveling already. Stacy was going to find herself tossed unceremoniously out into a snowbank beside her car and, really, wasn't that what she deserved?

"Aren't you his nanny?" McAllister demanded. "That's who I was expecting."

"I'm Stacy," she said, drawing in a deep breath. "Stacy Murphy Walker." Now would be the perfect time to say who she really was and why she was here.

Tell him the rest of it. But her courage was failing her. So much easier to focus on the baby!

"Uppie? Pwweee?"

And it did feel as if this baby—and maybe Kiernan, too—really needed her. And it felt as if she needed to be in this house that cried for a Christmas tree and a family to encircle it.

She reached into the playpen. The baby wound his chubby arms around her neck, and she hoisted his surprisingly heavy weight. He nestled into her and put his thumb in his mouth, slurping contentedly.

"I'm not exactly your nephew's regular nanny," she heard herself saying, "but I'm sure I can help you out. I'm very good with children."

She told herself it wasn't precisely a lie, and it must have been a measure of McAllister's desperation that he seemed willing to accept her words.

He regarded her and apparently decided she was a temp or a substitute for the regular nanny, which would also, conveniently, added to the bad roads, explain the delay in her arrival. After scrutinizing her for a moment, he rolled his broad shoulders, unfolded his arms from across his chest and looked at her with undisguised relief.

"I'm Kiernan McAllister."

"Yes, I know. Of course! Very nice to meet you." She managed to get one arm out from under the baby's rump and extended it, not certain what the protocol would be for the house staff. Did you shake the master's hand?

He crossed the room to her and took her extended hand without a second's hesitation, but she still knew extending hers had been a mistake. She had felt his hand already as he helped her from the chaise in his bathroom.

Despite the fact that his hand was not the soft

hand of an office worker or of her comrades in writing, but hard and powerful, taking it felt like a homecoming.

And if she thought the mere sight of his lips had posed a danger to her, she could see his touch was even more potent. A homecoming to some secret part of herself, because something about his hand in hers sizzled and made her aware of herself as smaller than him.

And feminine. Physically weaker. Vulnerable in some way that was not at all distressing, though it should have been to a woman newly declared to total independence and a hard-nosed career as a freelancer.

She yanked her hand out of his and felt desperate not to give him the smallest hint of her reaction to him. "And just to clarify, is your nephew Ivan or Max?"

"Max. I just like to call him Ivan."

Stacy looked askance at him.

"As in Ivan the Terrible," he muttered.

She could feel disapproval scrunch her forehead—a defense against the electric attraction she felt toward him—and something like amusement crossed McAllister's features as he regarded her, as if he was not even a little fooled.

Annoyingly, the light of amusement in his eyes made him look, impossibly, even more attractive than before!

"But his name is really Max." He cocked his head. "I guess that works, too, if you think about it. He's Max everything. Max noisy. Max sleepless. Max filthy, at the moment. He's just over a year. A horrible age, if there ever was one."

"He's adorable," she declared.

"No. He's not in the least."

"Well, he is right now. Except, he might need changing—

"Never mind! If he needs *that,* you *have* arrived in the nick of time. And while you look after it I will do the manly thing, and go look after your car. You can change his nappy and then be on your way."

Well, there was no need to tell him the truth if she was leaving that quickly!

He made the declaration of assigning them duties with such abject relief that Stacy tried to bite her lip to keep from laughing.

It didn't work. It was probably, at least in part, a

delayed reaction to her accident, but a little snort of laughter escaped past her clamped lips. And then another one.

McAllister glared, and more laughter slipped out of her. It seemed to her it was the first time since the disintegration of her relationship that she had had anything to laugh about.

The baby chortled, too, and it made her laugh harder.

"Sorry," she said, trying to bite it back. "Really. Sorry."

Here she was, an imposter in a complete stranger's home, so it must be nerves making the laughter bubble within her. Whatever it was, the more she tried to repress it, the more it burbled out of her, free.

"Are you laughing *at* me?" Kiernan McAllister, master of the house, asked her dangerously.

"No," she said, through giggles. "No, of course not."

"I don't believe you."

"All right," she gasped, wiping an amused tear from her eye, "it does strike me as a little funny that you would be afraid of a baby's diaper."

"*Fear* is completely the wrong word."

"Of course. Completely."

"I'm quite capable of doing whatever needs to be done."

"Yes, I can see that."

"I have been doing what needs to be done. And will continue to do so after you've gone back to Vancouver. You can report to my sister that I am more than a match for a baby."

She nodded. A giggle escaped her. The baby chortled. "So, we've settled it," she said, striving to be solemn. "It's not fear."

Kiernan McAllister glared at her, then the baby, then her again.

"*Aversion* is probably a better word. Not to Ivan himself, but to what Ivan can do."

"Do?"

"Doo."

"Oh." She caught his meaning and tried to bite her lip against the deepening of her laughter. It didn't work. A new little snicker escaped her.

"It's Murphy's Law," he said, frowning at her snicker. "In the changing-a-baby department, I learned something very quickly. I've always been a quick study."

That she did not doubt! "And what did you learn?" she asked.

"Anything that can go wrong, will."

She really did laugh then, not even trying to hold back. McAllister glared at her but could not hide his relief that the stinky baby was in her arms and not his.

Still, he squared his shoulders and said firmly, "You can help me with this one thing, and I will look after your car. Then you can leave."

And without another word, casting her one more warning look that said he was without fear, his chin tilted up at a proud angle, he turned on his heel and left the room.

"And that," she explained to Ivan, "is your uncle, the warrior."

CHAPTER FIVE

KIERNAN COULD HEAR the nanny's light laughter follow him out of the room. Despite the fact it was directed at him, the sound was as refreshing as sitting beside a cold brook on a hot afternoon.

And besides, she was right, and it probably was funny. He was a man who had a reputation for not being afraid of anything. From daring business deals to bold adventures, he had always tackled life pretty fearlessly.

At great cost, a voice told him, but he turned it off, savagely.

He went down the hall and into his bedroom to get dressed. The scent of the nanny—like lemon drop candies—tickled his nostrils. Why was he so aware of her?

When she had picked Max up, the look on her face had been completely unguarded. And she had looked radiant. It had been a Madonna-with-child moment, breathtaking in its purity. And it had moved Stacy Murphy Walker from button cute to beautiful in a stunning blink of the eye.

Kiernan had been taken by surprise by how cute the nanny was from the moment he had plucked her out of her car.

Stacy was not what he'd expected from a nanny at all. What he'd expected was someone like that famous nanny on television: stout and practical, certain of her own authority in the baby department, possibly bossy. Or perhaps, he'd expected an older woman with gray hair in a neat bun, and granny glasses.

What he had not been expecting was a young woman with dark chocolate coils of hair, skin as pale as the inside of a white rose petal and astounding green eyes, as deep and moody as the waters of a mountain pond. He had certainly not expected the nanny to show up in a toy car, whimsical red shoes and skirt that, given how conservative it was, made his mouth go dry.

Attractive women in his world were the proverbial dime a dozen. He'd dated models and actresses, as world renowned for their looks and style as he was for his business acumen.

Somehow, next to her, those women didn't seem quite *real.*

It wasn't just that the nanny was smart that set her apart, though it was more than evident she was, because he'd been around and dated plenty of very smart women, too, business associates and CEOs.

Again, in a very short time, the nanny had made them seem not quite real.

It was because of that moment in the great room, when he had watched her look around with such wistfulness, it felt as if he had seen straight to her soul. And then when she had picked up the baby...radiance.

McAllister had experienced many of the wonders of the world. He had frolicked on beaches and conquered mountain slopes, and ridden zip lines through the rain forest. He had seen lions in the jungle and ridden a camel through the desert.

He had been at the premieres of movies and plays, attended symphonies, eaten at some of the best restaurants in the world and sampled some of the most exquisite wines. He had shared exhilarating adventure and great moments with friends.

And still for all that each of those experiences

had given him that incredible feeling—the sensation of being alive tingling along his very skin—McAllister did not feel as if he had ever experienced anything quite as pure as the radiance that lit the nanny's face when she picked up the baby.

Why was he so stunned by his reaction to her? Because, he realized, he *had* reacted. It was the first time in a year that he had felt a stirring of interest in anything.

But worse, he had been totally caught off guard by the way the look in her face, even her mention of how a Christmas tree would be in his great room, had filled him with a sense of yearning.

Yearning.

He had not allowed himself to feel that since he was a child, when every single thing you hoped for just set you up for huge disappointments.

Simple yearnings back then: *normal* topping his list.

Kiernan shook himself. This was *not* him. Of course, the circumstances were no doubt to blame for the lack of discipline he was exercising over his own mind. Twenty-four hours of terror at the hands of his nephew, ending with the crashing sound of the nanny's car, and then having to rescue her from the garden had shaken his well-ordered world ever so slightly.

He had gone into rescue mode, bringing his defenses—already battered by the unexpected tribulations of caring for a baby—down yet another notch.

It seemed impossible that only yesterday, Kiernan had been in a completely different world. He'd been in his boardroom at a presentation being given by one of his top associates.

Mark had been one of his best friends, once. Now, he could barely look at him, because he had been there that day, a witness to Kiernan's worst moment, a moment of colossal and catastrophic powerlessness.

Mark was talking about a new real estate development, a tower that combined retail outlets, offices and condos on a piece of property Kiernan's company, McAllister Enterprises, had recently acquired in a posh and trendy downtown neighborhood of Vancouver.

Kiernan had willed himself to focus on Mark. To pay attention. Kiernan was, when all the fancy titles were taken away, still the boss. He needed to care.

His attitude was probably why rumors were beginning to swirl that he had put the company up for sale.

His gaze had drifted out the window to the typical fall coastal weather. The skies were leaden, and raindrops slid, like plump drops of mercury, down the floor-to-ceiling glass of the boardroom window. Through a maze of office buildings and a haze of low cloud, he could just see the jutting outlines of the mountains.

A year.

It had been almost a year to the day.

They said time healed all wounds, and for a while, Kiernan had clung to that, like a man lost at sea clinging to a single bobbing piece of wood.

But the truth was that he'd felt the agony as sharply as the day it had happened. There was a dark place within him, contained, but it felt as if it was taking every bit of his strength to keep the lid on it.

If he ever gave up, if he let the lid off what had been in him since the day his friend died, it would ooze out, sticky and black, like melted asphalt. It felt like it would ooze out and fill him, bit by bit, until there was not a bit of light left.

"Mr. McAllister?"

He'd started. His personal assistant, the ever-competent Miss Harris, had come into the room without him even noticing. Then she'd been at his shoulder, leaning over, whispering something about an urgent matter needing his immediate attention.

"Mr. McAllister?"

Miss Harris had *that* look on her face. It was the same look he saw on his sister's face and on the faces of his business associates, his staff, his colleagues, Mark. Concern, these days tinged with exasperation.

Kiernan interpreted it as: get with it. Wake up. *Come back to us.*

But he was not sure he could, not when it was taking everything he had to keep the lid on the box within him that contained enough darkness to completely obliterate light.

Relieved to be leaving the boardroom, and Mark, who looked at him with sadness he could not stand—he nodded his apologies, got up and followed Miss Harris out the door.

Miss Harris's voice sounded as if it was coming from underwater. *Left him here...were you expecting him...you forgot to tell me.*

They walked down the thickly carpeted hallways of his empire until they came to a smaller boardroom, across the hall from his own office.

He glimpsed inside the slightly ajar door to his domain.

Once, that room, with its priceless art, hand-scraped floors, fireplace and huge TV hidden behind a secret panel, had whispered to him smugly, *You have arrived.*

Now his victories felt hollow.

Miss Harris had opened the boardroom door and stood back to let him by. The smell that tickled his nostrils should have warned him he was not going to like what he found.

Still, his mind was struggling to categorize that smell against the backdrop of understated posh decor of this room when he passed through the door and froze.

There was a baby in one of those carrier things, the kind with the plump padding and the handle. The carrier thing was dead center of the boardroom table. The baby's furious kicking of his stout limbs seemed to be fanning the aroma into every corner of the room.

All babies looked identical to Kiernan, but he knew exactly who this one was—Max.

His cherubic facial features had nearly disappeared behind a wall of chocolate. At least, given the stench in the air, Kiernan hoped it was chocolate.

A secretary, no doubt pressed into unwilling service, cast a nervous look at Miss Harris, and at Miss Harris's nod, which Kiernan caught out of the corner of his eye, bolted from her seat and scurried past Kiernan with a whispered "Mr. McAllister."

The young secretary had an expression on her face comparable to a peasant woman escaping the hordes of Genghis Khan.

"What the hell?" Kiernan said. "Where's Adele?"

Miss Harris stared at him. "She left him. She said she arranged it with you."

His sister, Adele, could not seriously think he was in any way suited to be a caregiver to her baby!

She had not arranged anything with him! Kiernan realized things slipped his mind these days, but he knew this was not one of those things. He would never agree to take Max, and Adele knew that, too.

But they were approaching that sad anniversary. He did remember Adele saying she needed some time to herself.

He did remember agreeing with her.

"What exactly did she say?"

"Something about you taking him to the cottage in Whistler," Miss Harris said, consulting her ever-present notepad. "For a week. And not to worry. She's sending a nanny up to meet you there tomorrow."

He suppressed a groan and smelled a rat, as well as the other things in the room. Adele was plotting, using her child to try to get him back to the land of the living.

Her trust in him seemed entirely undeserved, especially when he reacted to the Max's screwed-up face.

"What are you doing?" Kiernan asked Max sternly. *Here,* he added silently.

But in the end, he had packed the baby into the car seat Adele had provided, texted her a stern *no nanny* while he still had cell service and driven to the cottage, because he knew how much he owed Adele and this baby.

It was his fault his sister did not have a husband, his fault the baby did not have a dad.

Still, it was hard to believe he had committed to looking after the baby only twenty-four hours ago.

It felt like a different lifetime.

And he was so exhausted it had made him vulnerable to the radiance in the surprisingly lovely nanny's face.

Now, bending over her car, already disappearing under a heap of white from the heavily falling snow, he brushed at the tires and looked at the tread, annoyed. They weren't even particularly good *summer* tires.

He was annoyed his mind was still on her, despite the fact he was out here and had things to do. He tried to figure out exactly what it was in her face that had triggered something in him.

And then he identified what that something was. When she had been able to visualize a Christmas tree in his great room, when she had lifted that baby?

He had felt hope.

Of course, she would not carry a burden of guilt the way he did. His fault, entirely, that he and his brother-in-law had been there that day.

And when he relived that moment, which he did often, of that wall of snow sweeping down on them? He was always aware that he could or should have done something different. He was always aware that it *should* have been him instead of the man who had so much more to lose, who had left the world with a fatherless baby.

Somehow, McAllister's genuine and startling enjoyment of a pretty girl's radiant face felt like the worst threat of all.

After all, wasn't hope the most dangerous of all things?

So, here was the question. Did he walk toward the light he had seen in her face? Or did he walk in the other direction as quickly and as firmly as he could?

Away, he decided. He was, above all things, good at making decisions. He made them quickly and decisively, and he never looked back.

He was unsticking her car and sending her on her way. He frowned at the drifting snow on the driveway. It would have to be plowed before anything else happened. The plowing was contracted, and he was surprised they had not been yet.

But they might not know he was in residence, which would make his driveway a low priority. He would call them right away.

Even when it was done, what would await on the public roads?

Okay, *he* would drive the car to Whistler and grab a cab back. Stacy had already shown, in spades, she could not be trusted in these driving conditions. Except what to do with Max during all this? Was the baby seat transferable to her car? Did he want to be out on these roads with Max?

It proved to be a moot point, anyway. After spending more than an hour pitting his strength and wits against the snow and ice and the summer tires, and almost succeeding in banishing the nanny from his mind, he could not get her car unstuck.

At first his irritation was monumental, but then a light went on. No! It was a good thing. After he called the plow company, he could call a tow company and have the car towed all the way to

Whistler for her, with her in the cab of the truck with the driver. He could be rid of her—and her sunshiny visions of Christmas trees in *his* great room—and he would not have to feel responsible for her safety.

Kiernan was actually whistling as he went back through the front door of his house and stomped snow off his boots.

He came through to the great room and stopped.

This was exactly what he was protecting himself against! Stacy had spread a blanket on the floor in front of the fireplace. The baby sat here, Buddha-like, his chubby face wreathed in smiles, his attention on the nanny. She was sitting across from him, on the blanket, her legs tucked underneath her, oblivious to the fact the skirt was riding up to reveal even more of those rather delectable legs.

She hadn't even noticed Kiernan's arrival.

Because she had another blanket over her head. As he watched, she lifted up a corner of it, and cried, "Peekaboo."

Max screamed with laughter, rocked back and forth and looked like he was going to fall over.

Her hand shot out from under the blanket and supported the baby.

"Aga!" he screamed at her.

Apparently it meant again, because Stacy disappeared back under the blanket. The baby held his breath in anticipation.

"Peekaboo," she cried.

Max went into paroxysms of laughter. Her laughter joined his.

For all the parties Kiernan had held here, filling this room with important people, rare wines and exquisite food prepared by an in-house chef, his house had never once felt like this.

Kiernan stared at them as if in a trance. That weakness whispered along his spine again. That longing.

For normal. For the thing he had never had. Home.

Something made her glance up, and when she saw him standing there, Stacy pulled the blanket off her head and leaped to her feet, yanking down her skirt. Her hair, crackling with static from the blanket, reminded him of dark dandelion fluff.

"Oh," she said, embarrassed, "I didn't realize you were there."

The baby was frowning at him and yelled his indignation that the game had come to an abrupt end.

Easily, as if she had been born to do it, she scooped up Max and put him on her hip. "I was just thinking of seeing what you have for him to eat," she said.

"Don't bother. You aren't staying." This came out sounding quite a bit more harsh than he intended.

"Oh," she said, looking hurt and baffled by his words, just more evidence she had to go. "You got my car unstuck, then?"

"No," he snapped. "I didn't. Not that I would let you drive if I had."

That chin went up. "That is not up to you!"

"I have to arrange for the driveway to be plowed. And then I'm calling a tow truck. He can tow you all the way to Whistler and you can ride with him."

"But—"

He held up a hand. "It's not open for discussion."

Now, as well as her chin sailing upward, her eyes were narrowed, but she had the good sense not to challenge him. Obviously she knew her driving skills were not up to the steadily worsening conditions outside.

So, that settled, he went to the phone. And picked it up. And closed his eyes against what he heard.

Which was absolutely nothing.

The storm had taken out the phone line. There was going to be no plow. And no tow truck. Not in the foreseeable future, anyway.

In fact, Kiernan's foreseeable future held a form of torment that he was not sure how to defend himself against.

As if to prove it, Max, annoyed at the abrupt end of his game and the nanny's attention not being focused on him, curled a chubby fist in her hair and yanked hard.

"Hey," Stacy said, "don't do that!"

Max yanked harder.

"I told you he was not adorable in the least," Kiernan said, and went to untangle the baby's determined fist from Stacy's hair.

In doing so, he tangled their lives just a little more together.

CHAPTER SIX

"IVAN, LET GO."

Kiernan's voice sent a shiver up and down Stacy's spine—the man could be deliciously masterful—but the baby was not impressed.

Glaring at his uncle, Max wrapped his fist more tightly with her hair.

Kiernan strode forward, and now both their hands were in her hair.

"Don't hurt him," she said.

"I'm not going to hurt him." Kiernan snapped, insulted.

But the dilemma was obvious: without actually forcing the baby to let go of her hair, he was not going to voluntarily give her up.

"Try distracting him," she suggested.

"How?"

"Can you make a funny face?"

"No!"

"A noise?"

"Such as?"

"I don't know. Try a choo-choo train. Or a duck! Maxie, do you like ducks? Quack, quack?"

She was sure the little fist slackened marginally in her hair. Stacy wished she had a camera to catch the look on Kiernan's face, that he, one of Canada's top CEOs, had just been asked to quack!

Instead of quacking, Kiernan reached into his pocket and took out his keys. He jingled them enticingly toward Max, who let go of her hair instantly and reached for the keys.

"Baby 101," Kiernan said. "Distraction. Do they teach you that in nanny school?"

That brought her other dilemma into sharp focus. It was, of course, the perfect opening to let him know that she was not a nanny. But now that they were snowed in together—trapped really—wouldn't it just make everything worse if she chose now as the time to let Kiernan know she wasn't exactly a nanny?

He didn't even have the option of throwing her out at this point. Nor did she have the option of volunteering to leave!

Her father had always said, *Murphy, my love, when you are given lemons, make lemonade.*

And that was exactly what she intended to do, right here and right now.

"I need to get the baby something to eat," she said. "And then he needs a bath. After that, he'll probably be ready for bed."

"Humph, he's never ready for bed. Let me show you what Adele left for food for him."

It was a turning point, because Kiernan seemed to resign himself to the idea she was staying. The fact that it was out of his control must have made it a little more palatable to him because, while she opened the baby food and prepared a bottle, he threw together some snacks for the adults.

After they had all eaten, she tackled the bath. To her surprise, Kiernan insisted on helping.

"He's bigger than you think," he said of his nephew. "And he's a slippery little character when he's dry, never mind wet."

Stacy found herself in his master bathroom again. This time, Kiernan flipped on the fireplace without being asked.

For her enjoyment, she couldn't help but wonder, or for the warmth of the baby?

Either way, the experience became wonderful. The fireplace glowing softly, Kiernan's strong hands holding the baby upright, Max gurgling and splashing while she scooped water over him with a cup.

She knew that this good working relationship wouldn't be happening if she had admitted her true identity. It would be better, she decided, for the good of the baby, if she just didn't say anything.

After the driveway was cleared, she could light out of there with no one the wiser. And she would drive her own vehicle, too!

By the time they were done, they were all soaked, but the baby was wrapped in a thick white towel and cuddled sleepily against his uncle's chest.

Stacy was not sure she had ever seen a lovelier sight than that little human being nestled so trustingly against one so much bigger and stronger.

Even the normally stern lines of Kiernan's face had softened, and in the warm glow of the fireplace the scene wrenched at her heart.

"What a beautiful father you will make someday," she said softly.

The look was gone instantly, and Kiernan glowered at her. "I do not have any intention of *ever* being a father," he snapped.

"But why?" she asked, even though it clearly fell into the "none of her business" category.

The look he gave her confirmed it was none of her business. "I'll go get your bag out of the car," he said stiffly, obviously not wanting to spend one more second than necessary with a woman who had spotted father potential in him.

Kiernan didn't just go get her bag. He went out and inspected his driveway, listened hopefully for the sound of a coming plow, but the night was silent. It was the kind of deep, deep silence that did not allow a man to escape his own thoughts.

What was going on in his house? He had just bathed a baby in front of the firelight, and enjoyed it, too.

No wonder Stacy was under the false impression he might make a good father someday.

He hated it that those words had triggered that thing in him, again.

Longing.

A yearning for something that would never be.

He remembered as a kid getting the odd glance into other people's lives, a friend inviting him home for dinner, the unexpected treat of a ski trip from his best buddy's mom and dad one Christmas.

Swooping down the hill, he had felt freedom from everything. But after? Eating with that family and playing board games with them and watching them talk and tease each other on the long drive home?

He had wanted what they had as much as he had ever wanted anything. He had learned the hopelessness of such feelings at the hand of his own father, who had been furious with him for accepting the gift of the trip, an affront to his pride, and he had screamed at Kiernan.

His father was a man he tried not to think about.

A man whose brutishness he had distanced himself from with every success, a man whose shadow he had seemed to escape when the rush of adrenaline was filling his every sense and cell.

Kiernan would never be a good father.

He was convinced it was something you learned, a lesson he had most definitely missed in life.

Though, a voice in him whispered, his sister seemed to have overcome those challenges. It could be done. There was hope.

But he hated it that he even wanted there to be hope. Hated it. And it seemed as if it was her fault, and even though they were stuck here together, he vowed to keep his guard up, find his own space, avoid her.

When he came back in the house, Stacy was sitting on his couch, legs tucked up underneath her, flipping through a book. It had gotten dark outside, and she had turned on a light and sat in its golden glow, unaware what a picture she made.

He recalled again the amazing gatherings hosted in this room, beautifully dressed people, swirls of color and motion, tinkling glasses and laughter.

Despite how much he liked it here, and the good memories he had, Kiernan was aware that, like his condo in Vancouver, his cottage lacked that little *something* that made it feel like home.

Apparently, that little something was a woman making herself comfortable on his couch! The scene was one of homecoming.

Stunned, he felt his decision to avoid her completely dissolving like sugar hitting hot water. Well, he did have her overnight bag, which he had found in the backseat of her car. What was he going to do? Drop it at her feet and bolt?

Really, it would be embarrassing for her to figure out she had rattled him.

"I brought in your bag. Are you okay sharing the guest room with Ivan the Tyrant?" At her nod, he said, "I'll put it in there. Where is Ivan the Tyrant?"

He realized it was blessedly quiet in his house. He tried to tell himself that was probably what he had appreciated at a subconscious level, as much as her presence on his sofa.

"Max is sleeping. You might want to leave the bag there for now rather than risk waking him."

He dropped the bag at his feet as though it was burning his hands. "Seriously? He's sleeping?"

"He wasn't awake very long. When I dug through his bag of things I found his soother and a stuffed toy he called Yike-Yike."

"That thing with eyes on it that looks like an overripe banana?"

"That's Yike-Yike."

Kiernan tapped himself with his fist in his forehead and groaned. "I should have figured that out. Where he goes, that thing goes!"

"Exactly! Within minutes of having both in his possession, he was out like a light. It seems early for him to go to bed, but I think he's managed to wear himself out—

"Not to mention his poor uncle!"

"—and I really think he could make it through the night. All of your problems with him crying and not sleeping and eating properly had to do with his distress over that. Bad enough, in his mind, that Mommy left. But no Yike-Yike?"

"Baby hell," Kiernan murmured.

"Exactly.""

He said a word he was pretty sure you weren't allowed to say around babies. Or their nannies.

"Did you get enough to eat?" he asked.

"Yes, thank you."

There. No reason to stay here in this room with her. None at all. He could retreat to his bedroom. But he didn't.

"Does the fireplace in here use real wood?" she asked wistfully.

"Yeah. I didn't want to light it with Ivan on the

run." *Get away from her,* Kiernan ordered himself. But the wistfulness in her face stopped him.

It was such a small thing that she wanted. Not like the things he had once wanted. He could give this to her. No one could have ever given his dreams to him.

Could a woman like this? He shook off the thought, more than annoyed with himself. Another reminder to get away from her and the spell she was casting. But now he'd offered to light the fire!

"I'll light it for you, if you want."

"Oh, no," she said, and blushed. "That's way too much trouble."

It was that blush that sealed it for him. "No, no trouble at all." And he found himself opening the damper and crumpling paper and setting kindling, striking the match.

In no time, the fire was crackling cheerfully in the hearth.

Now retreat, he ordered himself. But he didn't. He said, "I've got this contraption that supposedly you can pop corn in the fire. You want to try it?"

"Yes," she breathed with genuine enthusiasm, as if he had offered to put up a Christmas tree.

Well, what the heck? They were stuck here. Together. Entertainment was limited. Why not?

Stacy realized she should have said no to this. She should have wished him a polite good-night and retreated to her room. But she just wasn't that strong.

She joined him at his counter, and they eyed the open-fire popcorn contraption together. They took it to the fire and took turns shaking it vigorously as per the instructions.

Just when it felt as if nothing was ever going to happen, the popcorn began to pop. First one or two kernels, and then rapidly, like a machine gun going off.

"We put too much in," she said as the hinge sprang free and popcorn began to spill into the fire. It smelled terrible. A few unpopped husks exploded into the room with the briefest whistled warning and more velocity than she could have dreamed possible.

She dropped the popcorn maker, and he took a firm hold of her elbow and shoved her behind the couch, shielding her with his own body, protection of those who were smaller and physically weaker than him coming as naturally to him as breathing.

They tried to muffle their laughter so as not to wake the baby, while the popcorn flew through the air around them.

When they were sure the fireworks had finished, they came out from behind the couch.

He surveyed his living room with shock.

She giggled. "I've heard of popcorn ceilings," she said, "but never popcorn floors."

And then the laughter died. "Thank you for protecting me," she said.

He looked at her, and suddenly it seemed very still. Almost against his will, he reached down, tilted her chin up, scanned her face, looked at her lips.

"Do unexpected things always happen around you?"

"It's the old anything-that-can-go-wrong thing," she said, but her voice was husky and neither of them was laughing.

Awareness sizzled in the air between them. He dropped his head close to hers. He was going to kiss her!

* * *

Stunned, she backed away from him. This was a lie. She was living a lie! She couldn't let it get more complicated than it already was.

She turned on her heel and ran down the hall.

"Hey, Cinderella," he called mockingly, "You are leaving your slipper."

But she had more in common with Cinderella than she ever wanted him to know. Both she and Cinderella were both pretending to be people they were not.

Kiernan watched her disappear and gave himself a shake. Had he nearly kissed her? What on earth did that have to do with the strategy of avoidance he had planned?

Crazy things were happening in this house. The popcorn all over the floor was a testament to that. Nearly quacking for her earlier was a testament to that. Crazy things were happening in his head, too, and he didn't like it one little bit.

He was strong.

Stronger than strong.

He always had been. That was why he had survived. That was why Adele had survived.

But all his strength, he reminded himself bitterly, had not been enough to save Danner.

And that's what he needed to remember, before he tangled his life with anyone's. He was not the stuff happy families were made of. And even if he was, all his strength could not do what he would most want to do.

Protect from harm.

Kiernan gave his head one more rueful shake and began to pick up scorched popcorn from his living room floor.

And the fact that he smiled when he remembered huddling behind the couch with her only reminded him he had been weak when he wanted to be strong.

And so, as one day stretched into two and they remained marooned, he made himself be strong.

He was polite. And helpful with the baby. And aloof. If watching her interact with Max and making herself at home in his house gave him pleasure—which it did—he did not let on.

And when the snow finally stopped, he practically raced outside. If he could get her car free before the plow arrived, he was one step closer to being rid of her. And her laughter. And the way she shook her curls to make the baby coo with delight.

It would be good for him to get outside and do the manly thing! But, an hour later, he was no closer to freeing her car.

Though he did have a plan!

"So, how did it go with my car?"

He had promised the manly thing, and he was not going to admit defeat.

"Still stuck, but I think we could get it out together." What did doing anything *together* have to do with avoiding her?

"Well, the baby's napping, so now would be perfect. I'll just grab the monitor."

"I'm pretty sure it's an easy fix. It just needs two people, one to drive and one to push. Despite my desire to hold you captive—"

He realized he had said that to make her blush, too, and she did.

"—because of your gift with Ivan, looking after the car before he wakes up would be good. Because once he wakes up?" McAllister wagged his eyebrows at her. "Guess what? It's all about him."

"Typical male," she muttered.

That made him frown, because he was pretty sure he heard the faint bitterness of one who had been betrayed in there. Was that the shadow he saw in her eyes sometimes?

Well, how could that be anything but a good thing, that she had no illusions about the male half of the species?

"You are so right," he said. "We are a colossally self-centered, hedonistic bunch. You'd be better not to pin your hopes to one of us."

CHAPTER SEVEN

"You don't know the first thing about my hopes," Stacy said quietly. She had given him entirely the wrong impression when she had imagined a big family gathering in this very room. She had given him the wrong impression when she had told him he would make a good father. She had given him the wrong impression when she had leaned toward him that night of the popcorn and nearly accepted his kiss.

He couldn't avoid her, of course, and he hadn't. But she had felt the chilly lack of connection.

But just underneath that, something simmered between them, as if a fuse had been lit and the spark was moving its way toward the explosive.

She was so *aware* of him when he was in the same room. The same house. The same space. She was aware of loving the way he was with

Max, loving the way he was willing to do what needed to be done without being asked.

Kiernan McAllister regarded her thoughtfully for a moment, his gaze so stripping she felt as if he could see her soul.

He was dressed in a beautiful down-filled parka, the fur-lined hood framing his face. Beautifully tailored slacks clung to the large muscles of his thighs, the look made less formal by the fact the slacks were tucked into snow boots.

How could a man look every bit as sexy dressed as he was now as he had when he was dressed in nothing but a towel?

But McAllister did. In the parka and the snow boots, he looked ready for anything. Very manly, indeed.

"Unfortunately, Stacy, I think I do know a bit about your hopes."

"And?" she said, bracing herself for his answer.

"Your career choice says quite a bit."

That was a relief. What he assumed was her career choice was telling him about her. Her hopes and dreams, as battered as they were at the moment, weren't really showing on her face.

"Who wants to look after other people's children?" he said. "Except someone who loves children and dreams of having their own? Probably by the bushel."

The truth was she had planned for three, someday.

It would be the perfect time to tell him she was not who he was expecting, that she was not a nanny at all. Instead, she found herself frowning at him. "Are you saying *you* don't love children?"

"I already told you, I don't plan on being a father."

"That doesn't answer my question."

"I don't even like children."

She snorted.

"Ah, indignation. As if I've announced I don't like puppies. Or Santa Claus."

"Actually, it's not indignation, Mr. McAllister—"

"It's a little late for formality."

Oh, boy. "You aren't a very good liar."

"Excuse me?"

"The baby frustrated you, and you were at rope's end, but I could tell you would have protected him with your life, if need be. Maybe that's not *like*. And over the last few days, when you see something that needs to be done, you just step up to the plate and do it. That seems suspiciously like more than that. Like love, perhaps."

He was glaring at her, and then he shrugged a big shoulder dismissively.

"Whatever, Miss Poppins," he said. "We need to look after the car before His Majesty wakes up. Have you got a winter jacket somewhere?"

"Just my sweater."

"I'll find stuff for you."

The "stuff" he found was mostly his and so, a little while later, Stacy was following him out into the darkness of a still-snowing night, dressed in a jacket that came down to her knees and that tickled her nostrils with the pine scent of him. He had found her a hat that that looked like something a turn-of-the-century trapper would wear. It was too large and kept falling over her eyes. Thankfully, his sister had left snow boots here that fit her.

Really, she should have stopped him at *Miss Poppins.*

And confessed to her true identity. For about the hundredth time in three days, she knew she should have, but she just couldn't.

Because, she had the certain knowledge, that as soon as she did it would be over. She was pretty sure she had not banked enough gratitude that he was going to grant her an interview. Especially now that she had seen him so clearly and called him a liar.

She was the liar. And revealing that to him was going to cause terrible tension and they were trapped here. It would not be good for the baby!

Even if, by some miracle, the truth came out and he did grant her an interview, *then* it would be over.

And somehow she did not want this little adventure to be done. What had he said to her earlier?

You might want to keep in mind, for next time, to try and steer into the spin, rather than away from it. It goes against everyone's first instinct. But really, that's what you do. You go with it, instead of fighting it.

So, what if she went with this? Rode the momentum of the spin instead of fighting it? Let go of her need to control, just for a little while? Isn't that what she'd been doing for the past few days?

It seemed to her that since the second she had

wound up with her bumper resting against that fountain, her life held something it had not held for some time. Surprise. Spontaneity. The potential for the unexpected.

When unexpected things had happened to her before, it had been so in keeping with Murphy's Law. They were always bad.

Expecting an engagement ring and being invited to shack up being a case in point.

Dylan had guffawed when she had said that, apparently more loudly than she had thought.

Shack up, Stacy, really? What century is that from?

One where people made commitments and took vows and wanted forever things instead of temporary pleasures.

Then, she had done something totally out of character. She had dumped her wine all over his head, and yelled at him, "What century is that from?"

Unfortunately, her worst moment ever in keeping with Murphy's Law, had been recorded by someone in the restaurant with a smartphone, who had been alerted to turn it toward her by her rising tone of voice.

And then that moment had been posted on the web.

But all that was in her past. Now was now. And, as ridiculous as it seemed, Kiernan McAllister, the man who appeared to have everything, seemed to need something from her.

As did that baby. And so Stacy was going to take his advice.

You might want to keep in mind, for next time, to try and steer into the spin, rather than away from it... It goes against everyone's first instinct. But really, that's what you do. You go with it, instead of fighting it.

"Oh, Stacy," she murmured inwardly, "what kind of predicament have you gotten yourself into?"

A dangerous one, because if what she had experienced so far—his nearly naked self, fresh out of the hot tub—wasn't his idea of 100 percent manly, she was in very big trouble, indeed!

"Okay, put it in Reverse," Kiernan shouted from the front of her car.

Stacy sat in the driver's seat of her car, peering out from under her hat at Kiernan. She had the window rolled down so that she could hear instructions from him. She was already glad for the winter clothing, especially the mittens. The baby monitor was on the seat beside her as she clenched on the steering wheel. It was very sensitive. She could hear Max's soft, sleepy purring above the sound of the engine.

She contemplated the delightful if somewhat surreal quality of her life.

One of the most powerful men in the business world was getting her car unstuck from his front garden as she listened to a baby sleep.

After scowling at her summer tires, he had settled right into it.

It had been a very pleasant experience so far watching him wield a shovel, digging out the tires of her car, one by one, spreading gravel underneath.

"Give it some gas."

She did. The tires made that whining noise. Kiernan put his shoulder against the front bumper of her car and pushed.

Manly, indeed!

Kiernan did look 100 percent man. How it was even possible for him to look more manly than he had in his swim trunks baffled her, but he did and heart-stoppingly so. Of course, sharing a house with him had made her superaware of him: his scent, how his hair looked wet from the shower, the shadow of whiskers on his face late in the afternoon.

Now the winter clothes made him look rugged, tough, 100-percent Canadian male, ready for anything. He had long since dispensed with the gloves, which were lying on the ground beside him. His brute strength rocked her car, and for a moment she thought he was going to be able to push it free, but it seemed to settle back in the ruts.

She let off the gas.

"Try rocking it between Forward and Reverse."

Stacy did this, she could tell from the way his arms crossed over his chest and the expression on his face—part aggravated, part amused—that she was doing something wrong.

"Sorry," she called out the open window.

He came and leaned in the window. His breath touched her like a frosty peppermint kiss. "You really aren't great at this, are you?"

She looked at him from under the hat. Great

at what? The whole man/woman thing? No, she was not.

"You're a snow virgin!" he declared. "It's a good thing it's not a full moon. We sacrifice snow virgins at the full moon."

He was teasing her.

She had never been good at this kind of banter, but she reminded herself to go with the spin.

"To what end?" she asked breathlessly.

"Appeasing the god, Murphy."

She laughed then, and the smile that she could have lived for—and that she could have told a zillion more lies to see again—tickled the sensual line of his lips.

He leaned in her window, right across her, and took her gearshift. "Put in the clutch."

He was so close his whiskers nearly scraped her cheek. She wasn't even breathing. He snapped her gearshift into Neutral and backed out of her window, leaving her feeling like a snow virgin very close to melting.

He went back around to the front of the car and showed off his manliness by shoving some more but to no avail.

"I have an idea," she called. "You drive. I'll push."

"Sure," he said cynically.

"No, really. I'm stronger than I look."

He looked skeptical, but by now he apparently had figured out she was not going to get the gas or the gears right to rock the car out of the spot it was in.

"Don't push," he instructed. "I'll see if I can get it out without you."

She could see he knew a great deal about cars. He rocked the car back and forth gently, but it would come to the same place in the ever-deepening rut her great winter driving skills had created.

She went around to the front of her car and pushed.

"Hey," he called out the window, laughter in his voice, "you are not helping. It is like an ant pushing on an elephant."

She ignored him and pushed.

"Try just putting some weight on it."

She threw her weight against the bumper, and when that didn't work, she sat on the hood. Apparently that was the ticket, because suddenly the wheels caught and the car rocketed backward.

She fell off the hood and rolled through the snow. Her hat fell off and her mouth filled up with the white stuff.

He got out of the car, raced to her and got down beside her.

"Are you okay?"

"I'm fine." She spit out some snow, and he brushed it from her lips.

"Are you always so accident-prone?"

"Murphy's Law," she reminded him.

"Ah," he said. "And we have failed to appease him." He held out his hand, and she took it— she was becoming too accustomed to this his-hand-in-hers stuff—and he helped her to sitting. He found the hat, shook the snow out of it and clamped it back on her head.

"Your car is unstuck. Let's get in out of the cold."

"I don't feel cold," she said. "You go in if you want to. I'd like to stay out here for a while. Snow virgin that I am, I want to enjoy this for just a bit longer. This might be the closest I ever get to my winter holiday."

He smiled at that.

Boldly she said, "How would you recommend losing snow virginity?"

His smile faded and he stared at her, and if she was not mistaken, his eyes went to her lips. She could feel her heart beating too fast again. She was inordinately pleased that he seemed flummoxed by her question. Then something burned through his eyes that felt too hot for her to handle.

"I will make a snow angel," she decided quickly.

He looked relieved by her choice. Obviously angels and whatever wicked thoughts he was having did not go together.

He was having wicked thoughts about her? It was dismaying...in the most wonderful way.

Still, she lay back down in the snow, splayed her hands over her head and swept the snow with her tights-clad legs.

"How does it look?" she asked.

"Angelic," he said, something dry in his tone.

"How do I get up without wrecking it?"

He seemed to ponder this and then, with a trace of reluctance—a little close to those wicked thoughts to risk touching her—he reached down. She took both his arms, and he swung her up out of the angel she had made in the snow. He let her go instantly.

"It's lovely," she declared. She stood surveying her handiwork with pleasure and leaned down to brush at the snow that clung to her legs.

"Lovely," he murmured, and she shot him a look. Had he been looking at her?

"It would be great to get Max outside tomorrow," she decided. She opened her car door and checked the monitor. The baby was still sleeping soundly. "Maybe we'll build a snowman."

What was she doing talking about tomorrow? She needed to tell McAllister the truth now. But somehow she was not so certain what truth was. Wasn't there a truth in this moment under inky skies in the way he had murmured *lovely* after watching her brush the snow from her legs?

Wasn't there truth in the way their breath was coming out of each of their mouths in little puffs that joined together to make a cloud?

Weren't these truths as profound as any other truth she had ever known?

"The snow will be gone by tomorrow," he said.

"Really?"

"It's stopped snowing, finally, and the weather has warmed. It won't take long."

He was right. When she looked up at the dark sky, wisps of clouds were moving away to reveal a bright sliver of moon and pinpricks of starlight. It was beautiful.

"It's just an early-season storm," he told her. "The snow won't stick. It'll melt by tomorrow."

Tomorrow the magic would be gone. *Then* she would tell him the truth. There would be an escape route. Max didn't have to be affected. But tonight?

"I better build a snowman now, then," she said.

"Seriously?"

"I'm a Vancouver girl. You never know when you might have another chance."

McAllister stooped, picked up a handful of snow and squeezed it. "It is perfect snow for that."

Was he going to help her? Her astonishment must have shown in her face.

"You don't have enough muscle to lift the balls on top of each other," he said, as if he needed an excuse to join her.

"Hey!" She scooped up a handful of snow and

formed it into a ball. "I have muscles aplenty! I just got the car unstuck!"

"Single-handedly," he said drily. "No help from me."

"Very little," she said, and then she realized *she* was teasing *him*. In a moment of pure and bold spontaneity, she tossed her snowball at him.

He dodged her missile effortlessly and stood there looking stunned. Something twitched around the line of his mouth. Annoyance? Or amusement? Annoyance. His mouth turned down in a frown.

She thought he would tell her to knock it off or grow up or get real.

He was the CEO of one of the biggest companies in Canada. You didn't throw snowballs at him.

She held her breath, waiting to see what he would do.

Gracefully, he leaned down. She saw he had scooped up a handful of snow of his own. His gloves were still lying in the snow over by where her car had been, but that didn't seem to bother him at all. With his bare hands, not looking at her, he slowly formed the snow into a ball.

Finally, he looked at her, held her gaze.

A smile, not exactly nice, twitched around the line of that beautiful mouth.

She read his intent and, with a shriek, turned away from him and began to run through the mounds of beautiful white snow.

CHAPTER EIGHT

"DON'T!" SHE CRIED. She glanced over her shoulder.

His too-large jacket flapped around Stacy's legs, making it impossible to attain the kind of speed necessary to outrun the missile he let fly.

The snowball caught her in the middle of the back. Even with the padding of the winter coat, it stung.

"I'm taking that as a declaration of war." She laughed, pushing back the sleeves of the jacket and scooping up more snow. She took careful aim, her hat slipping over her eyes, and to his shout of laughter, she pulled the hat back up just in time to see her snowball miss him by a mile.

She scooped up more snow and formed it into a hurried ball. She hurled it at him. He moved his head to one side and it whistled by his ear.

Deliberately, he walked over and retrieved his gloves. He was already tired of the silliness.

No, he wasn't. With his hands protected, it was evident he was just getting started. He stooped and grabbed a mitt full of snow. He began to shape a rather formidable looking snowball.

"There's no need to be mean about it," she told him over her shoulder, already running again.

"You're the one who declared war!"

And then he was running after her, his legs so much longer than hers that he was gaining ground fast. She was going to have to outmaneuver him. Stacy scooted around the fountain and through the shrubs. She ducked behind her car.

Silence. She peered over the hood.

Sploosh. Right in her face.

"If you surrender now, I'll show you mercy," she shouted at him, wiping off her face and ducking behind the car to pick up more snow.

"Me surrender to you?" he asked incredulously.

"Yes!" she shouted, forming a snowball, her tongue between her teeth.

"Surrender? Lass, I'm of Scottish ancestry. That word is not in my vocabulary."

She peeked out from behind the car, aimed, let fly. She missed.

"Glad I didn't wave the white flag," he said with an evil grin.

"I'm just sucking you deeper into enemy territory."

"You're terrible at this," he told her.

"What's that called, when you play billiards badly to suck the other person in, and then place a bet and show what you can really do?"

"Hustling," he said.

"Maybe that's what I'm doing."

"I'd be more convinced if you knew the word for it."

"All part of the hustle," she assured him. She let fly a snowball that caught his shoulder and exploded with satisfactory violence. She chortled happily. "See?"

A missile flew back at her. She ducked behind her car, and it shattered harmlessly behind her. Silence. She waited. Nothing happened.

She peeked around the front fender. He had been making ammunition and had a heap of snowballs in front of him.

She reached inside the still-open door of her car, picked up the baby monitor and held it up.

"Be careful," she said, "you don't want to get this wet."

"It's waterproof. You can take it into the bath-tub." He let fly with six in a row and, as she peeked over the car, he tucked six more in the crook of his elbow.

She shoved the monitor in her pocket as he came running toward her, and burst out from behind the car at a dead run.

With a whoop he was after her. They chased each other around the circle of his driveway. As he threw snowballs, she ducked behind shrubs and the fountain and her car until they were both breathless with laughter and dripping with snow.

"Okay," she called, laughing, when he had her backed up against the fountain and his arm pulled back to heave a really good one at her, "I surrender. You win."

"What do I win?" He kept his arm up, ready, if she did not offer a good enough prize.

She licked her lips. If she was just a little bolder, she would offer him a kiss from the snow virgin.

Instead, she backed away from the intensity building between them. She pulled the monitor out of her pocket. "This! A completely water-proof baby monitor."

"Thanks, but no thanks."

"Okay, you win an opportunity to build a snow-man!" she said.

"Sheesh. I was at least hoping for hot choco-late."

"Take it or leave it," she said.

"Pretty pushy for the loser." He tossed the snowball away. "I'll take it, but only because it's obvious to me you can't be trusted with making a snowman. You can barely make a snowball, and a snowman is the same principle, only multiplied."

"I'm anxious to learn whatever you want to teach me," she said.

For a moment the intensity sizzled again be-tween them, white-hot into the frosty evening. His eyes locked on her lips and hers on his. She felt herself leaning toward him as if he were a magnet and she was steel.

He stepped back from her. "No, you aren't," he said gruffly. "I wouldn't want you to learn from me. There's something innately sweet about you. My cynicism could demolish that in a second."

Of course, he was saying that because he thought she was a nanny.

This was where lying got you.

"Maybe my sweetness could demolish your cynicism," she said.

"It's an age-old question, isn't it? Which is stronger? Light or dark?"

"Light," she said without hesitation.

He snorted but took some snow and squished it into a ball in his hands. Then he set it down, got on his knees and pushed it. Snow began to glue to the ball magically, and it got bigger and bigger.

Her skirt was not made for this kind of activity!

But what the heck? She had tights on. Following his instructions, tongue caught between her teeth, she lowered herself to her knees, too, and began to push her ever-growing snowball across his snowy driveway.

When she glanced over at him, he was straining against a huge snow boulder! It was so big he had his back against it and was pushing backward off his heels.

"That's big enough! Kiernan, it's bigger than me!"

She realized, stunned, his name coming off her

lips felt like an arrival at a place she had always dreamed of being at.

This is not truth, Stacy warned herself of the game she was playing. But she was not sure anything in her life had ever felt truer than this, playing in the snow under a night sky with Kiernan McAllister.

She was just going with the spin, instead of fighting it.

"Just a little bigger," he said. "Come help me push. It'll be just the right size by the time we get it over to the fountain."

He was far more ambitious than she was. It took them pushing together, shoulders touching, to wrestle it into place where her car had rested a few minutes before.

"You're an overachiever," she gasped, stepping back to admire their handiwork and, surreptitiously, him.

"Yes, I am," he said with complete pleasure.

He moved over to the ball of snow she had been working on. "Break is over," he told her, and side by side they pushed that one into place, too.

It took both of them to hoist the second ball

on top of the first. There was much panting and laughing and struggling.

The snowman's head was the smallest of the three balls, and by now the snowman was so tall Kiernan had to lift it into place himself.

They stood back. The snowman was a good eight feet tall, but sadly blank faced.

"This is the problem with all that ambition," Stacy said. "He's so big we can't reach his face. He needs a hat. How are we going to get up there?"

"I already have it covered," Kiernan said.

"You're going to go get a ladder?" she asked.

"Ha! I'm going to be the ladder!"

She contemplated that for a moment. That sounded dangerous in the most delicious way. She saw he was moving snow to get at the rocks underneath, and she joined him.

"Do you have a carrot for his nose?" she asked.

"Oh, sure, in my back pocket. That's why I'm digging for stones."

"This one's perfect for the nose," she said, reaching down and picking up a pure black rock that he had exposed. "And these for his eyes! And these for his mouth!"

He was watching her, amused. "I think you have enough." He crouched down on his haunches.

"Here, hop up. Don't drop the rocks."

He tapped his shoulders. *As if dropping the rocks would be the most of her problems!*

She hesitated for only a moment before climbing on.

He lifted her with ease, and she found Kiernan McAllister's rather lovely neck between her legs. He grabbed her boots and held them against his chest. She had been unaware of how soggy and cold her clothing had become until she felt his warmth radiating up through her wet tights.

He pretended to stagger sideways, and she gripped his forehead and giggled when he yelped, "Hey, get your fingers out of my eyes."

She moved her hands and he staggered back in front of the snowman.

"Quick," he said. "I don't know how long I can hold you. You must weigh all of—what—a hundred pounds?"

Trembling, and not just from cold, Stacy put the face on the snowman. The nose rock was perfect, and if the smile was a little crooked, that was understandable. She snatched the hat off her own head and placed it on the snowman's.

"Okay," she called. "We're done."

But he didn't put her down. Instead he galloped around the yard, pretending he was staggering under her weight, ignoring her pounding on his shoulders and demanding to be put down at once.

Finally, he went down on one knee, but her dismount was clumsy, and she caught his shoulder, and they both went to the ground in a tangle of limbs and laughter.

Then the laughter died and the silence overtook them. They lay there in the snow, looking up at the stars.

"I haven't laughed like that for a long time," he said quietly.

"Me, either."

"Why?"

She hesitated, but from sharing the house and the baby duties there was a sense of intimacy between them. "Oh, life has taken some unexpected twists and turns. I've kind of felt just like I felt on your driveway—spinning out of control."

"A man," he guessed, with a knowing shake of his head. "Failed marriage?"

"No."

"Broken engagement?"

She winced.

"Ah."

"We never got that far," she confessed. "I just thought we were going to."

"Ah, that imagination-collides-with-reality thing again," he said, but with such gentleness she felt her heart break open wide.

Suddenly, she wanted to tell him all of it. She felt safe with him. Ironically, though she was posing as someone else, she felt more herself than she ever had. And she wanted him to know the truth about her.

"It wasn't just a man," she said quietly. "I became on orphan at sixteen."

It was terrible to feel this way: that she could trust him with anything on the basis of a few days trapped in a house with him.

A few wondrous days, where she felt she knew more about him than she had ever known about anyone. Still, could she continue to blame that hit on the head for the removal of the filter for socially acceptable behavior? You did not unload your personal history on the most powerful man you had ever met.

Except he felt like the Kiernan she had seen bathe the baby.

And who had built a fire for her. And protected her from popcorn missiles.

And who had lent a hand whenever he saw something that needed doing. It was ironic that she could not tell him who she really was, and the more she could not tell him that the more she wanted him to know!

"They died. My grandmother, my mother, my father, my little brother. It was a car crash. My entire family," she whispered.

"I'm so sorry," he said. His voice was velvet with sincerity, and he reached out to tuck a strand of hair behind her ear. He touched her cheek for a moment before he let his hand fall away, something in his face telling her he was as surprised by that gesture as she was.

She had been dating Dylan for three months before she had told him any of this. Of course, he had never looked at her like that...

"I'm sorry," she stammered. "I don't even know why it came up."

"Thank you for telling me," he said. "I feel honored."

"And you?" she whispered, needing more from him, needing the intimate way she felt about him—the trust she felt for him to be reciprocated. Even if she did not deserve it.

The snow had stopped. By tomorrow, there was a chance she would be gone from here. She could not stay once the snow was gone. She needed to take some piece of him with her. "Kiernan, what has kept the laughter from your life?"

He rolled a shoulder uncomfortably but said nothing.

"The death of your brother-in-law?" she asked softly.

He cranked his head and looked at her. "And what do you know about that?"

"Oh, Kiernan, you are a very public figure. The whole world knows about that."

He sighed and looked back up at the stars. "It's been a year. That's why my sister needed some time right now. People say time heals all wounds, but I am waiting for evidence of that."

"I'm so sorry," she said. "It was a terrible tragedy."

"How did you get over it?" he asked.

"I guess I hoped to have again what I once had before," she admitted, and it felt as if her heart was wide-open to him. "After my disaster with Dylan, I've given up on it."

"No, you haven't."

"I have," she said stubbornly.

"Then why can I so clearly see you surrounded by all your beautiful babies, and a man worthy of you? Someday, you'll look back on it, and be glad it happened. You'll see that he was a complete jerk and that you deserved better."

A hopeless feeling came over her. There was that imagination again. Because somehow it seemed Kiernan might be the better man she had waited for. But she knew she did not deserve him.

"As a matter of fact, I've decided to put my wildest imaginings aside," she said stiffly.

"No, you haven't," he said softly. "Because you know what is possible. You know what it is to be part of a family. You aren't imagining that part. And because you're not? You'll never stop looking. You'll never stop seeing what could be in rooms like my great room. I need to know, step by step, how you got through the loss of your entire family."

She could hear the desperation in his voice, and she knew how vulnerable he had just made himself to her. He was asking her to help him.

Stacy took a deep breath and contemplated the stars. When she spoke, her voice was husky and hesitant.

"At first, I didn't feel as if I would even survive, not that I wanted to. I went from having this wonderful family into foster care. Thankfully, it was only for a year until I finished high school. I'm not sure you get over it. You get through it.

"Eventually, it was being around the kids in foster care that woke me up. Many of them had never had a loving family, or anyone who genuinely cared about them. At the risk of sounding corny?"

"What else would I expect from Miss Poppins?" he teased, but his tone was so gentle it was like a touch.

"Being around those troubled kids showed me what to do. Find somebody to help. That's what saved me. I started to go to university to get a degree in counseling. Unfortunately, I couldn't afford to finish the program. I became involved in starting a charity—Career and College Opportunities for Foster Kids—and I think that has pulled me through my darkest moments."

"I've never heard of that charity," he said.

"Unfortunately, neither has anyone else. We just don't have the know-how, the expertise, to get it really rolling."

"I'll give you the name of someone who will help you."

See? Despite all the evidence to the contrary, sometimes your wildest imaginings could come true.

"How did you get by?" he asked. "After you dropped out?"

"Thankfully, I had another gift that came in handy."

The other gift was writing. Was now the time to tell him? He was offering someone to help the charity under a false impression of who she was, after all.

But to lose this moment of closeness so soon after she had laughed for the first time in such a long time felt like more than she could bear.

"Your gift was with children," he said. "That's how you became a nanny."

Instead of responding to that, Stacy said, "In

time, instead of focusing on the loss, I was able to feel gratitude for my family, and for the time I'd had with them. Every gift I have been given comes from the love they gave to me. Maybe you'll feel that, eventually, about your brother-in-law."

The silence was long and comfortable between them. She realized the days of being trapped together had made them friends, had created a bond between them with astonishing swiftness.

"He was more than my brother-in-law," Kiernan said, finally, softly. "We were best friends. Funny, when I first met him, I was prepared to dislike him. When my sister announced she was bringing someone home, I practically met him at the door with my saber drawn, prepared to give all kinds of dire warnings about what would happen to him if he hurt my sister.

"But Danner was just the best guy." A long silence, and then Kiernan said, "I wish it could have been me, instead of him."

CHAPTER NINE

"OH, KIERNAN," SHE said.

That *feeling* she had of experiencing truth at its deepest and finest intensified. She saw that he was a man who would see the protection of those he loved as his highest calling.

And that he had failed in it.

He gave her a look that forbade her sympathy. "He had a wife. And a baby. It would have been better if it was me."

She did not know what to say to that. She thought a deeper truth was that these things were not for mere men to decide, but she felt it would sound trite to say that in the face of the enormous pain he had trusted her with.

And so instead of saying anything, she took off her mitten and slid his glove off and took his bare hand in hers.

She held it.

And he let her. And it felt so good and so right

to lie there on their backs in the snow, looking at the stars through the clouds of their own breath and feeling intensely connected by the fact they both knew the burden of intense loss.

Then he let go of her hand.

"You officially have lost your snow virginity."

She knew he was trying to change the subject, to move to lighter ground, but she felt a need to stay in this place of connection just a bit longer.

"I have built a snowman once before," she said. "With my dad. While everyone else was cursing the snow, he was out playing with us. He could make anything fun."

She could feel his hesitation, but then his hand was once again in hers, warm against the cold of the snow around them and the chill of the night.

Warm in a world that was so cold sometimes it could freeze a person's very heart.

"You're lucky for that. I wonder if that's where your dream of having a winter holiday comes from? Wanting to recapture that moment of childhood magic?"

His perception warmed her as much as his hand in hers. "Do you have moments like those, Kiernan, pure magic?"

He snorted. "Not from my childhood."

This was what being a reporter with some counseling background had taught her, that silence was a kind of question in itself. She suspected Kiernan was a man of many barriers, but for some reason, these playful moments, these few days of being snowbound, had lowered them.

"It was probably more like the kind of family kids you ended up in foster care with came from. My dad was a drunk," Kiernan said softly. "He abandoned the family when I was about twelve."

"That's terrible," she said, "and so, so sad."

"Believe me, it was a blessing. Anyway, that's why I was meeting my sister's boyfriend at the door. By default, I was the man of the house."

"Oh, Kiernan," she said softly.

"That's why my sister and I always go away at Christmas. Someplace warm and beachy and non-Christmassy. To outrun the memories of him, I guess. Adele—that's my sister—she says that's why I'm allergic to relationships."

It was a warning if Stacy had ever heard one. But it was also an admission of something deeply private.

Her hand tightened in his despite the warning. She thought he would shake her off now, but he didn't.

"You must be very proud to have accomplished all that you have," she said.

"Proud?" He was silent for a long time. "I used to be."

"And now?"

"Now I feel as if I wasted precious moments on a clock that I did not know was ticking a relentless countdown, pursuing things that did not matter."

In that moment, for the first time, Stacy realized Dylan, her ex, might have been right about her when he'd let her go from her job. It had seemed too coincidental, in light of the fact their relationship had just ended, but now his words came back to her.

Maybe Dylan had been right, Stacy thought. She just didn't have the instincts for this.

"You're a good writer," he'd told her, *"but you're no kind of reporter. You don't have the guts for it. There's no daring in you. And you have to be able to be a bit ruthless in some circumstances."*

A ruthless person—a true reporter—would have asked right now if the rumors of McAllister Enterprises going up for sale were true.

But Stacy could not bring herself to do anything more than be in the silence of his pain and regret with him.

"Your hands are freezing," he said, as if that was why he hung on to them instead of letting go. The warmth of his own hands was absolutely delicious on her icy flesh.

"Don't feel sorry for me," he said dangerously. "I'm sure it is also the reason I'm so driven to be such an overachiever in everything I do, including building snowmen."

Still, holding her hand, he got up on one elbow and looked down at her, and for one breathless moment she thought he was going to kiss her.

Instead, he seemed to realize who they were—who he was and who she was, and he shook the snow off himself, let go of her hand and stood up.

"Do you always have this effect on people?" he said. "Draw their secrets from them?"

She didn't know what to say, so she said nothing at all.

The things he had told her felt sacred. Her desire to tell his story to get her career on track was leaving her like the wind leaving a sail.

He stared at her for a long time, and she was sure that he was going to recognize the danger of what was happening between them.

And perhaps he did. But instead of walking away from it, he walked right toward it.

His hand tightened on hers. He lifted it to his lips and blew the warmth of his breath into her palm. It spoke—sadly, she thought—of her past relationship with Dylan that Kiernan McAllister warming her hands with his breath was the most romantic thing that had ever happened to her.

He was right. For the first time, she felt grateful for the fact her relationship had gone sideways. In her eagerness to create a family again, she had been able to gloss over the fact her relationship had been missing a certain *something*.

It felt dangerously as if that *something* was in the air between her and Kiernan, more dazzling than the stars in the sky above them.

And then a sound split the night, deep, rumbling, jarring.

"What is that?" she asked, her eyes wide. "An earthquake?'

He pulled his hand from hers and shoved it in his pocket. "It's the snowplow," he said. "He's clearing the driveway."

It was over, she thought. As quickly as it had begun, it was over. She could already feel the distance gathering between them, could see the distance in his eyes.

He turned quickly away from her and strode toward the house, leaving her behind.

"I bet the phone is working," he said. "I have all kinds of business to catch up on."

He was letting her know it was completely out of character for him to have been frolicking with the nanny in the snow. He knew the intimacy of the past few days was creating a grave danger between them, and he was doing the wisest thing. Backing away from it.

Returning to his world.

And she would be returning to hers.

Kiernan retreated to his master suite. He contemplated the evening: getting her car unstuck, chasing her through the snow pelting her with snowballs, the huge snowman that now graced his front yard.

He did not behave like that.

Nor did he lie on the snowy ground, the cold coming up through his jacket, telling all his secrets, telling a near stranger things he had told no one else.

Exhaustion, he excused himself. He had not slept properly since Max had arrived.

He had never abandoned his company quite so completely as he had in the past twenty-four hours.

Though he knew he had been abandoning it mentally for months. He knew about the rumors that he was selling out. Not true. He probably should contain them, but the company was not publically held, so he had no one to answer to, no stock prices plunging because of the rumors.

Still, he checked his phone. It was working, finally.

He knew Adele would be frantic and despite the fact it was late, he called her. She did not answer, so he left a message saying the phone had been out, a fact he was pretty sure Adele would have determined for herself when she could not get though.

"Everything's fine," he said in his message.

He told her Max was thriving and that the nanny had arrived so all was well, despite them having been snowed in.

And then he did something he *never* did.

"Hey, sis, I love you."

He hung up the phone slowly. What did that mean, anyway, that he'd included that? His sister knew, of course, that he loved her. But he rarely said things like that.

He thought about the snowball fight, and the snowman, and lying in the snow, looking at the stars. Had the words been to reassure his sister? Or did it reflect how he really felt? Softer in some way than he had felt a few days ago. More open.

Was it possible he was happy?

Was it possible his happiness was related to the nanny?

"Don't worry," he growled, setting the phone beside his bed, stripping down and climbing between the sheets. "Life has a way of snatching those moments away."

For months—possibly even for a full year, going to sleep had been a torment for Kiernan. Those were the moments he tossed and turned and endlessly relived moments that could not be undone.

But tonight, he fell asleep instantly. In the morning, the phone rang, and it was his sister. When he hung up he knew just how right he had been.

Life *did* snatch those moments away.

CHAPTER TEN

STACY AWOKE AND stretched, luxuriating in her surroundings. Sleeping in the bed had been like sleeping on a cloud. The room was that beautiful seamless mix of elegant and rustic that she had seen in the rest of the house.

Last night, being careful not to disturb the baby, she had dug through her things until she had found the bathing suit she had brought in case she wanted to avail herself to the facilities at the Whistler hotel she had booked.

A moment of searing guilt when she had found the suit: the hotel she had booked to write a story about Kiernan McAllister.

Obviously, after he had shared so deeply last night, writing about him was out of the question now. He had trusted her.

The thought sent a shiver up and down her spine. How many opportunities had she had to set the record straight with Kiernan, to tell him she was not a nanny?

She stared at the bathing suit. It was plain and black, made for swimming, not for sharing a hot tub with the likes of Kiernan McAllister!

She looked out her bedroom window. The clouds had drifted back in, blotting out the stars. It had started to snow again, heavily. She felt Kiernan's prediction of a melt was probably incorrect.

If she put off making her confession for a little longer, she would have an opportunity to play with the baby in the snow.

She was sure she would be able to talk Kiernan into joining them. The picture of them as a happy family unit filled her with bliss.

Getting into her pajamas—no more chosen for an encounter with McAllister than her bathing suit had been, Stacy crawled between the luxurious sheets and felt herself not just looking forward to tomorrow but feeling strangely excited by it.

She slept well and deeply and woke in the morning feeling that tingle of excitement, as well as feeling rested. She rolled over and peeped at the playpen.

It was empty!

The thought that Max might be old enough to get himself over those railings and out of the playpen had not even occurred to her! Would it have occurred to a real nanny?

She scrambled out of bed.

"Max!"

No answer. And no baby under the bed or in the bathroom or hiding behind the curtains. Her door was firmly closed. Surely, he could not have gone out.

Not even taking the time to avail herself of the luxurious housecoat that hung on the back of her bedroom door, Stacy flew down the hallway to the great room of the house.

"Max!" She had to shout over something roaring.

She skidded to a halt when she came into the room. Max was sitting on a blanket on the floor, surrounded by cookies. His uncle, in a housecoat like the one hanging on the back of her bedroom door, was sitting on the couch. He was at the controls of a...

She ducked as a remote control helicopter dive-bombed her.

Max chortled and pointed and stuffed another cookie in his mouth.

It was a happy scene except for one thing. The master of the house looked far from happy.

In fact, his mouth was set in a grim line, and when his eyes rested on her, there was something in them she didn't understand.

Contempt?

She looked down at her pajamas. All right. Surely he was used to something a little sexier than oversize white flannel with cotton-candy-pink kittens in the pattern. He seemed to have things under control—literally, since his hand was on the helicopter controls. She could duck back into her room and get dressed.

But then he would know she wanted to make a good impression on him. Erase that look of scathing judgment.

Come to think of it, there was no way *that* look was being caused by a choice in night wear!

"You should have called me," she said, coming into the room hesitantly, having to speak loudly over the whir of the helicopter. Had she slept right through the baby waking up? That meant Kiernan had come into her room. Had he watched her sleep?

Of course he hadn't. That would imply far more interest than she saw in his closed features this morning.

"I would have got up with him," Stacy said. And certainly she would not have given him cookies for breakfast.

Kiernan's expression only got darker.

"Because that's what nannies do?" he asked, his tone cool.

Stacy felt something inside her flash freeze at his tone. She said nothing, but she could feel herself bracing for the worst, her heart sinking.

"The phone was working last night," he said, his voice cool and grim. "I left my sister a message right away. Just a brief message. Don't worry. Ivan and I are fine."

Kiernan paused and stared at her so long and hard that she squirmed. "Cavalry has arrived," he finished, his voice full of menace.

Stacy held her breath. Kiernan looked away from her now, frowning at the helicopter, which had gone seriously off course while he stared at her. It was flying dangerously close to his price-less chandelier, and he corrected its flight path while the baby clapped.

"I told her the nanny was here."

Stacy wanted to flee from the look on his face, but instead she moved across the room and sank down on the couch beside him. He seemed to flinch as he moved marginally away from her.

"She never sent a nanny," he said, his voice a growl of subdued anger. "She wanted Max and I to have time together. She thought—" He stopped himself abruptly and shook his head. "Never mind. It doesn't matter what she thought."

"She thought it would be good for you," Stacy guessed.

Kiernan landed the toy helicopter on the coffee table. He put down the controls and flicked something. The whirring sound stopped, and the blades coughed to a halt. He ignored Max's shout of protest.

The silence was more unnerving than the noise had been.

"We're not talking about me right now," he said, and his tone was dangerous. "We're talking about you. So, if my sister didn't send a nanny, that begs a question, doesn't it?"

Stacy nodded, stricken.

"If you aren't the nanny," he asked quietly, his eyes dark with anger and accusation, "who are you?"

He put a very bad word in between *who* and *are*.

I'm the woman you threw snowballs at, and made a snowman for. That's what is true.

But she couldn't bring herself to say it.

"I never actually said I was a nanny," Stacy whispered.

"You implied it."

"Yes, I did," she said woefully.

"And you probably knew that I was desperate enough for help to go along without asking too many questions."

"I *did* want to help you."

He snorted.

"I'm sorry," she whispered.

"You could be arrested, you know."

She leaned her head back on the sofa and closed her eyes. She was trying very hard not to cry. The look on his face was one of utter betrayal.

"That would be just my luck," she said. "Of all the exciting things a person could get arrested for, I get arrested for impersonating a nanny." She was trying to hide the fact she was nearly crying with the attempt at humor, but she was pretty sure it was a fail.

Humor fail it would say on the internet, just as the post of her last evening with Dylan had said *proposal fail.*

"Don't try and charm me with your Murphy's Law talk," he said. "Just tell me who you are, and what you want from me."

"I'm a writer," she whispered.

He snarled, an angry sound from deep in his throat.

She shivered. "That sounds like a mountain cat, right before he attacks."

"Don't try and distract."

"All right. I'm a writer. I recently lost my job at *Icons of Business,* under very unfair circumstances."

"Lack of ethics?" he said silkily.

"No! You were right last night—"

She could tell he did not want to be reminded

of last night. "I made the mistake of dating my boss. Then it ended. I lost my job over it."

"If that's a play for sympathy, it's not working."

"I just wanted you to know everything I said has been true. Except for the nanny part. Which I didn't actually *say.*"

"Sure. You probably made that up about your family, just to wiggle in here. The pajamas are a nice touch. What's not to trust about pink kittens frolicking?"

She knew he was angry because she had wiggled her way not just into his home but, for a little while last night, right by his rather formidable defenses. That was what he was truly upset about—that he had trusted her and been vulnerable to her—and she did not blame him.

"That part about my family is true," she said, and felt her eyes smarting from the pain of trying to hold back tears. "Who would make up something like that? And everything I said about the charity is true. Please don't hold it against the charity."

He did not look like he believed her, and she realized her chances of him helping her were over. She could never ask him to be the honorary chair now. Even his giving her the name of somebody who would help her was gone.

Everything that could go wrong had, only she wasn't the victim. She had brought it totally on herself this time.

In a rush she said, "The only thing that isn't true is the nanny part. I was fired—"

"Unfairly," he said cuttingly.

"Yes, it was unfairly! My boyfriend was my boss, and when our relationship ended, guess what? I got fired!"

He looked totally uncaring.

She rushed on. "I'm trying to make a go of it as a freelancer. A friend from my old office phoned and told me where you live. I thought if I could get the story about the possible sale of your company, I could save my career."

"My company is not for sale," he said grimly, then tilted his head at her and smiled tightly. "No, wait. Maybe it is."

She ignored him and continued, her voice a near whisper, "And I guess I thought maybe I could get help for CCOFK at the same time.

"But then when I wound up in your flower bed, and my head was hurt, and the baby was here, I lost that initial opportunity to be up-front with you. It did seem to me you might need me. And that you'd throw me out if you knew who I really was and what I really wanted."

"Your lies were driven by pure altruism," he said cynically. "You thought I needed help with the baby. Very nice of you. And if all kinds of details about my life that I don't want anyone to know show up in print? That's just the price I pay for being helped, right?"

"I didn't actually lie," she said again, but she knew it sounded weak. "But I did misrepresent myself, and for that I am truly sorry. I'll get dressed and leave right away."

She had spoiled everything, even CCOFK's one chance of getting a much-needed boost. Filled with self-loathing, she scrambled up off the couch, but he caught her wrist and held her fast.

She tried to pull free, but he wouldn't let her.

"You're not going anywhere until you've signed a contract saying what you heard here, from me, stays here."

"That goes without saying," she said, tilting her jaw proudly.

"Sure, it does," he said coolly. "I have your word for that."

Well, could she really expect him to trust her? On what basis? That they had built a snowman together? Chased each other with snowballs?

She thought he had *seen* her, but now she could see she had wrecked everything.

"I'll sign whatever you want," she said with stiff pride, holding back tears. "You can get it ready while I go gather up my things."

She paused at the baby.

Max was looking between them anxiously. Now he looked at her and smiled, tentatively. "Upppeee? Pweeee?"

She cast a look at Kiernan's dark features, and then she didn't care what he thought about it. She scooped up that baby and pressed her nose into the sweet curve of his neck.

"Bye, Max," she whispered. The tears she had held back came when Max pressed both sides of her face with his hands and gave her a worried look.

"No bye!" he shouted imperiously. "No bye."

She buried her teary face deeper in Max's sturdy little shoulder.

"You *are* being a little premature in saying goodbye."

She whirled, scrubbing the tears with her pajama sleeve, and looked at Kiernan McAllister.

"You aren't going anywhere." His tone was cool and dangerous.

He stood up and came over to her. His grace was leopardlike and just as lethal. She forced herself not to turn with the baby and run. Instead, she stood her ground, knowing she deserved his censure. She had to crane her neck to see him. He towered over her.

"The roads are a worse mess than they were yesterday. It's on the news. Despite my driveway being plowed, there are accidents everywhere." Then his features hardened as he realized that could be interpreted as concern for her.

"My nephew, in a very short time, seems to have become attached to you. I think he's suffered enough losses. You will stay until I find a replacement for you."

Emotion warred in her. One was relief: obviously Kiernan did not think she was as terrible a person as she herself felt she was at the moment.

He would not trust her with his nephew if he felt she was really a criminal.

But the other emotion she felt was pure horror.

How could she stay here under these circumstances, with Kiernan bristling with dislike for her?

"How long will that be?" she asked, her voice barely more than a whisper.

Kiernan checked the date on his watch. "I have no idea. I've never been in the market for a nanny before."

"I can't stay here indefinitely." Under these circumstances? It was impossible. She would rather face roads with a whole winter's worth of un-cleared snow on them.

"Don't even act as if you have a choice," he warned her. "You are here until I tell you you may go? Is that clear?

CHAPTER ELEVEN

STACY'S MOUTH OPENED to protest. Of course, Kiernan could not force her to stay here. Still, she recalled her premonition when she had first turned toward his house. That it was not Cinderella's castle, but Beast's lair.

Was that just a few days ago?

It seemed as if it had been a lifetime ago, as if by playing in the snow and exchanging confidences under a starry night, she had changed in some fundamental way. Kiernan McAllister couldn't keep her here against her will!

"You can't—"

She started to say it but then snapped her mouth shut. He was not the one in the wrong here, she was.

And if it was sincere interest in this baby's well-being—and okay, Kiernan's as well—that had prevented her from telling the truth, those were the very things that would keep her here.

Not his order that she could not leave but her own sense of decency.

Whether he knew it or not, she had just been given a second chance to do the right thing. Do-overs were rare in life, and she was taking this one.

Kiernan came out of his home office, sniffing the air like a wolf who had caught wind of something he didn't quite understand. He'd managed to hide out in his office all day. Finding a nanny was a little more difficult than placing a call, Miss Harris had informed him an hour ago.

You had to fill out applications. You had to provide references.

You had to have a criminal record check, for God's sake.

It was one of those rare circumstances where it did not matter how much power, influence or money you had.

Finding a real nanny took time.

Why, he asked himself, did he feel as if he needed a nanny now? He'd insisted to Adele he didn't need one before.

The truth was, for all that he was giving an

appearance otherwise, he felt like an emotional wreck, unsure of himself in ways he had never felt before. He felt angry with Stacy and angrier with himself.

And it wasn't just about her *not* being the nanny.

It was about the hope that he had allowed into his life when he knew that was the most dangerous thing of all. He needed her to stay here until his disillusionment was complete. And then he needed a professional nanny to step quietly into her place and look after Max so he could lick his wounds without doing any harm to the baby.

He knew, after all, how harmful adults dealing with things could be on unsuspecting children.

Kieran was used to solving problems quickly and aggressively. He was used to knocking down obstacles that got in his way. He had found there were very few problems money could not solve.

But apparently the nanny agency was not budging from its position. No criminal record check, no nanny.

He had not even looked at the forms Miss Harris had faxed him to fill out so she could forward them to the Royal Canadian Mounted Police. Instead, he had started looking over the plans for that hotel/condo development in downtown Vancouver instead.

Stacy Murphy Walker could be the damned nanny until his sister came back.

And he wasn't hiding from her, either, as if he was scared of her.

Despite her wariness of Kiernan's scowling bad temper, Stacy seemed determined not to let that affect the baby at all.

Despite the horrible tension between them, his house was filled with happy sounds. Laughing. Lots of laughing. And singing. There was lots of baby talk.

Maxie, you are such a smart baby. And so cute. I'm falling in love with you.

Such was his aversion to hearing about Stacy falling in love that he had gone into his bathroom, ripped tissue into thin strips, which he had then rolled and stuffed in his ears.

Ears plugged, Kiernan vowed he was not going to be pulled into her world or her web. He didn't actually want to see Stacy laughing. Or singing. Or winning over that gullible little baby.

But now, just like that wolf, hunger was driving him from the safety of his den.

As soon as he opened his office door, scent smacked him in the face. His house smelled almost unbearably good, but that intensified his need to approach with extreme wariness. Good smells often laced the trap, after all.

He went down the hall stealthily, ready to retreat at the first sign of danger. He paused at his bedroom door. His bed had been stripped of bedding, and he recognized one of the smells that tickled his nostrils.

The washer and dryer, set back in an alcove in the hallway invisible behind doors, were running. Those scents were not of the kind dangerous enough for a manly man to run from, even if he was peripherally aware there was something about those scents—laundry soap and dryer sheets—that made his house a home.

Feeling even warier, he continued down the hall and came into the great room, where he stopped in the shadow of the hall and watched for a moment, undetected, to gauge the danger.

It looked very dangerous, indeed.

Again, his house looked transformed.

Wrecked but transformed. An abundance of toys were scattered hazardously over the floors.

A tent had been made—was that the goose-down duvet off his bed—between the coffee table and the couch. Max was under the shelter, babbling away happily to Yike-Yike.

Max had not entertained himself, not even once, since his arrival. They had gone through six sets of batteries on the helicopter.

Stacy was in the kitchen area of the great room. Kiernan realized how good this design was for parents—the sink faced the seating area, so a mother could be busy in the kitchen and still supervise the kids.

Not that he wanted to be thinking of Stacy as a mom.

And yet there she no denying she somehow suited for that very role. She was flitting from counter to sink, totally unaware of him. She was humming, and she had that disturbing look of radiance about her that Kiernan had first seen when she had picked up Max.

It occurred to him that instead of butting his head up against a wall looking for a new nanny, he should have been checking out her story.

Surely, someone who had experienced the kind of losses she claimed could not look like that?

Maybe what he thought was radiance was just heat. A stove timer went off, and she put on a pair of oven gloves and opened the oven door. As she turned back from the oven, hot pan in hands, her face was flushed.

Her hair had been pulled back, but a few strands had escaped captivity, and she blew one out of her eyes.

He had not made a sound or moved, but she suddenly went very still, the doe who had realized the wolf watched her, the prey becoming aware of predator. She looked at him.

"Hi," she said tentatively, hopeful, no doubt, that her flurry of activity was moving him toward forgiveness.

When he didn't say anything, she looked disappointed but moved on quickly.

"Can you put hot pans right on this surface?" she asked, giving a worried look to the countertop.

"What the hell are you doing?"

"I'm making things," she said, and then she beamed at him, still foolishly hopeful of his forgiveness. "Double ovens!"

She said that in a tone that most of the women

he dated would have reserved for a diamond tennis bracelet.

"You can bake cookies and pizza at the same time," she told him, with the kind of reverence that should be reserved for technological wonders like putting a backup camera in the tailgate of a truck or being able to stream live from the International Space Station.

Now that she had identified what was cooking, his senses insisted on separating the smells and categorizing them in order of their deliciousness.

He could smell chocolate chips melting and cheese bubbling, bread dough crust crisping.

"Are you trying to worm into my good graces?" he asked. Damn it. His mouth was watering. "Put those down, for Pete's sake, before you burn a hole through the oven glove."

"I just wasn't sure if I could set them right on the—"

"Yes!" He didn't expect his voice to be such a roar of complete frustration. She set the sheet down with a startled clatter.

Cookies.

Chocolate chip, just as his nose had told him.

"I had chocolate chips?" he said.

"Actually, an incredibly well stocked pantry."

There had been many chefs and caterers in this kitchen. Someone had set it up. Still, for all the good things that had been cooked in this kitchen, Kiernan was not sure the scents had ever been quite so tantalizing.

She turned back to the other oven and came out with a pizza, and not the kind you got at the deli section of the store, prefabricated, either.

"I didn't think you'd want to eat out of cans two days in a row."

It felt necessary to let her know he was in no way reliant on her domestic diva-ishness. "I usually order takeout. There are several really good restaurants in Whistler that will deliver."

"Oh, well, this is done now, if you're hungry. I'd hate to ask anyone to tackle the roads today."

Compassion for the delivery guy was not really a sign of a devious mind, his own mind insisted on pointing out helpfully.

He hadn't been aware just how hungry he was until she put that pizza on the counter, the crust golden, the cheese brown and bubbling.

He prevented himself, just barely, from running over there and starting to gobble it up like a starving creature.

"What were you doing in my bedroom?" he demanded.

"I just grabbed your sheets. I thought—"

"I don't want you to think. I want you to stay out of my bedroom."

"I'm making amends," she said stubbornly.

"A cleaning service comes in after I leave. I don't like having staff in my houses. And my feelings about having staff are private. And I don't want you poking through my things. You have enough ammunition on me. I don't need the whole world entertaining themselves with insights into how I live."

"I wasn't poking through your things! I took your sheets."

"No snooping through my drawers looking for fascinating insights into my life?"

"What kind of fascinating insights would I find in your drawers, for heaven's sake?"

She seemed to realize that could be taken two ways and the flush in her cheeks deepened.

"I once had a reporter ask me if I wore boxers or briefs."

"Well, that was bad reporting," she said, annoyed. "Because, believe me, big man that you are, your underwear is of absolutely no interest to anyone."

But her voice sounded strangled.

"You don't care to know?" he asked, taking wicked enjoyment in her discomfort, especially after that *big man that you are* crack.

"No!"

"Neither," he said.

She took a sudden interest in the cookies. She started taking them off the cookie sheet and putting them on a rack. They were obviously way too warm to be moved, crumbling as she touched them.

And she seemed totally unaware of it!

Save the cookies or enjoy her discomfort a little more? He could have both. He moved into the kitchen beside her and removed the utensil she was destroying the cookies with from her hand.

"There, put that in your story."

"There isn't going to be a story," she insisted. She tried to grab the utensil. "Why would I be making amends if I planned to go ahead and write about you?" she said.

He took a cookie off the sheet with his fingers, still holding the flipper out of her reach. He popped the whole thing into his mouth. "You're just trying to lure me into a false sense of security."

She looked annoyed—which was safer for him than the *radiant* look she'd been sporting as she juggled hot pans out of the oven.

But obviously, part of making her amends was biting her tongue, because she didn't voice her annoyance.

In fact, her voice seemed deliberately sweet as she responded to his just-as-deliberate nastiness.

"Well, now you can have nice clean sheets tonight, and while you're lying in them, you can think, *that Stacy is a much nicer girl than I thought. I don't think I will have her arrested for impersonating a nanny, after all. She's trying very hard to make things right. I may just forgive her.*"

In the battle of light and dark, she was not going to win! And she, he reminded himself, was the transgressor. For all that sweetness, she was the one who had behaved without integrity.

Though, he noticed uneasily, he could not bring himself to think of her as representing dark.

He knew that was his lot in life.

"I don't want to be lying in my bed thinking of you in any way," he said. "And I don't think you want me to be thinking of you, either."

She gulped. And blushed.

Which was exactly what he'd intended. No sense her thinking her *amends* were going to batter down his defenses.

Because they weren't.

He was aware he could forgive her—she'd been misguided. It was obvious to him, from the stripped beds to the tent for Max to the cookies coming out of the oven to the concern for the delivery guy trying to tackle the roads, that there was not a malicious bone in her body.

It was obvious to him that she was going to wear herself out proving that to him and that he should put her out of her misery now.

Maybe he could have forgiven her, but it seemed easier not to. It seemed to him she was the kind of girl who dreamed the kind of dreams he could not ever fulfill.

It was doubtful he could have even before the death of his friend.

After?

Not a chance.

"If I'm ever thinking of you in my bed, Stacy Walker? The last thing on my mind will be the clean sheets."

There. That should scare her right out of her annoying domestic efforts to make amends.

He went over to the counter, took a plate from where she had a stack of them and grabbed two. He filled one with pizza and the other with cookies. He had enough food to avoid her until his sister came home, since he had resigned himself to the facts he was not going to find a nanny and that he didn't really want to find one, either.

Some twisted part of him was enjoying this torment! He got in a parting shot.

"And if you are ever in my bed, the last thing you will be thinking about is clean sheets."

Her mouth opened, and closed, a fish gasping for air. But then her eyes narrowed, and she glared at him.

"You are absolutely right," she said in that same sweet tone of voice. "I wouldn't be thinking of sheets. I'd be thinking about the toilet paper in your ears."

They glared at each other. He fought back the compulsion to tell her it wasn't toilet paper and to rip the tissue paper earplugs out of his ears. He wouldn't give her the satisfaction!

CHAPTER TWELVE

KIERNAN HAD ALMOST made good his escape from Stacy when he heard the sound of a vehicle grinding its way up his hill.

Instead of turning toward his bedroom, he approached the front entry and looked out the window.

It was still snowing heavily and a cab was pulling up in front of the house. It slid in the identical spot that Stacy's car had slid in, narrowly missing where hers sat now.

"Are you expecting someone?" he called.

"Yes," she said. "My old boyfriend. I've been expecting him for months. I hoped he would realize the error of his ways, drop down on bended knee and beg me to come back to him."

Kiernan watched his sister get out of the cab.

He turned back toward the kitchen. Adele arriving meant Stacy was leaving. Since it should have been a *yahoo* moment Kiernan was taken a little aback at how he felt.

Protective.

Despite her effort to sound flippant, he realized she really had, in that wild little imagination of hers, played out her boyfriend's return to her and probably in excruciating detail, too.

Stacy Murphy Walker was leaving. What would it hurt to set her straight before she went?

"So, would you take him back?" he asked, juggling his laden plates and leaning his shoulder against the log pillar that separated the kitchen from the hallway.

"In a breath," she said.

"Why? He sounds like he was an ass."

"At least he wore underwear," she muttered.

"I never said I didn't. I just said I didn't wear boxers or briefs."

He could tell she wanted to ask what, but she didn't. She clamped her mouth in a firm line, and said, "Well, it's not as if we're interviewing you to be my boyfriend. There is going to be no boyfriend. I am going to be a dedicated career woman. I am going to devote myself to CCOFK."

"I thought you'd take him back."

"He's not coming back. It's a revenge fantasy."

"If it really was, when he got down on bended knee, you'd say no, not yes."

"Well, he's not coming back, so I have planned my life without him. Or anyone."

"Sounds lonely," he said.

"I'll get a cat."

He walked across the space that separated them. She backed up until she hit the counter with her behind and had no place to go.

"What are you doing?" she stammered.

He couldn't let her go without tasting her. He carefully set down the plates. He lowered his head to hers and took her lips in his.

In that second he knew everything that was true about her.

Every. Single. Thing.

And he knew something about himself, too. He hadn't insisted she stay here because of the roads. He hadn't insisted she stay here because of Max.

It was because of him. It was because she had succeeded, in a few short days, of doing what no one else had done. Breaking something open inside him. Something that *wanted* light instead of darkness…

The kiss deepened. Kiernan took his time exploring her lips as he felt her initial startled resistance melt. It was followed by a surrender so complete it felt as if she was dissolving into him, her slender, soft curves melding to his own harder lines.

Her hands moved from the counter where she had braced herself and twined around his neck, pulling him down to her.

There was something in her he had not expected. Sweetness gave way quickly to something more savage, more hungry.

He heard the front door open.

"Yoo-hoo? Anyone home?"

"Mama!" Max cried.

Kiernan yanked away from Stacy. They stood staring at each other, chests heaving. Her hair was mussed where his hands had tangled in it; her lips were swollen and her cheeks were flushed.

He turned from her and watched as his nephew exploded out from under his tent and headed down the hall.

"If there's a Triple Crown for babies," he said, raking a hand through his hair, trying for a casual note so that Stacy would not see how that kiss had shaken him, "he's going to win."

"What was that about?" she whispered. He shot her a glance just in time to see her touching the swollen swell of her lips with trembling fingertips. She was staring at him with wide eyes.

If his sister wasn't shaking snow off her coat in the front hall, he was pretty sure he would finish what he started.

But then he'd known his sister was coming when he had started, a safety net, in case he fell.

And Stacy was the kind of girl who could make a guy fall: straight into the wide pools of her eyes, straight into the softness of that heart. She was the kind of woman who could make a person who had lost hope entirely think that there was a chance. Stacy Murphy Walker had stormed his world, and it felt as if there was only one defense against that. The one he should have taken the minute he found out she was an imposter but hadn't. Stacy had to go.

"It was a gift," he growled.

"A gift? Your kiss was a gift," she stammered, but her eyes were narrowing dangerously. She was incensed, and he deserved it.

"Just letting you know," he said quietly, "you'll never be satisfied with a cat."

She touched her lips again.

"Or the old beau, either," he said.

He heard his sister coming down the hall and sprang back from Stacy just as Adele came into the room, Max riding in the crook of her arm, her cheeks sparkling from the cold.

And her eyes sparkling in a way he had not seen for a long, long time.

Adele looked at him and then at Stacy and back at him. He had the horrible feeling that Stacy's mussed hair and swollen lips—not to mention the glitter in those green eyes—were a dead giveaway. Adele knew exactly what had transpired between them.

"Stacy Walker, my sister, Adele. The reason you can leave now."

"Leave?" Adele said. "No one's going anywhere in that! The cab could barely make it from Whistler. I thought we were going to wind up in the ditch a dozen times. The roads were littered with vehicles. Your driveway was in the best shape of any road I was on today."

"I'll drive her," he said. He heard an edge of

desperation in his voice. He was pretty sure, from the way Adele's head swung toward him, she heard it, too.

When he had kissed Stacy it had been because goodbye was in clear sight.

Adele had a little smile on her face he didn't like one little bit.

"Yes, that's fine," Stacy said, her voice strained. "I'd have to come back for my car, though."

"I can have it delivered."

"That seems like a great deal of trouble," Stacy said, ridiculously formal, given that he had just kissed her. And she had kissed back.

"No trouble at all."

"Quit being so silly," Adele said.

Silly? He glared at his sister just to help her remember who he was, but she wasn't even looking at him.

"You aren't going anywhere," Adele said, offering her hand to Stacy. "I've been looking forward to meeting you. And even more so now that I saw the snowman! He's adorable. I just can't wait to get to know the woman who could convince Kiernan to make a snowman."

"How do you know I made it?" Kiernan demanded.

"It's eight feet tall, for goodness' sake. Who do you think I would think made it? Max?"

Adele put her nose against her baby's and said, "Mommy missed you so much, you adorable little winky-woo. I couldn't stay away from you for another minute."

He was pretty sure it was news of the imposter nanny, whom she was now greeting with the enthusiasm of a just discovered royal relative, that had brought his sister home.

Or maybe not.

When his sister looked at Max, despite all her losses, she had the same look on her face that he had seen on Stacy's. Radiance.

Or was it all because of Max? It had never occurred to him until this very second that maybe his sister had not been alone on her getaway.

"He's not..." he told Adele, stopping just in time from saying *winky-woo,* "an adorable little anything. He's a demanding little tyrant."

"Takes after his uncle, then," Adele said with a nod.

He'd had enough of her. "Look, I'm exhausted

and I need—Stacy needs to go." He felt he'd revealed way too much with that one, because Adele looked at him sympathetically.

"The morning is plenty of time to figure out who is going where. I've just been on those roads. I don't want you on them."

In her voice, he heard the thread of real fear, the understanding that life could change in an instant, in one bad decision. He had put that fear and that awareness in his sister; he had done that when he had failed to protect her husband.

"I guess we could figure things out in the morning," he conceded with ill grace, since he could clearly see an argument was going to get him nowhere.

"Good! That will give Stacy and I a chance get to know each other."

Adele and Stacy, these two ever so resilient women, getting to know each other?

He shot his sister a dark look, which didn't perturb her in the least, retrieved his plates of pizza and cookies and headed down the hall to his room.

If he closed his door with a little more force

than was strictly necessary, it was perfectly excusable.

Hours later he gave up on trying to sleep, because even with pillows over his head—he wasn't using toilet paper again—he could still hear them out there giggling away like old school chums.

A tap came on his door.

He quickly turned off his bedside light.

The door opened and Adele came in. "I saw the light from under the door."

He sat up and grudgingly turned the light back on. "What do you want?"

"You don't have to say that as if I'm some kind of traitor!"

"You knew she was an imposter! You're the one who alerted me that you hadn't sent a nanny at all. I'm surrounded by women who lie to me. What is the idea of saying you were sending a nanny when you had no intention of doing that?"

His sister made herself comfy on the edge of his bed.

"It was just hurting me so badly to see how Danner's death was affecting you, Kee. You seemed to be slipping further away every day.

And there was something sharp and cynical and angry about you that I had never seen before."

"That doesn't sound like someone anyone in their right mind would leave an infant with!"

"I knew you were in there somewhere. And I thought being around Max would force you to wake up, to be *here,* instead of in that dark place you couldn't seem to come back from."

"You're saying that in past tense, as though I have come back."

"There's a snowman on the front lawn," she said.

"That is hardly the miracle you are looking for, Adele."

"I need to tell you something," she whispered.

"What?" He was not sure he liked her tone of voice.

"Mark and I started seeing each other a while back. At first, it was just comforting each other over Danner. Sometimes, we'd talk about our mutual concern for you. Anyway, that's why I needed some time this weekend. I needed to make a decision."

"About?"

"Mark has asked me to marry him."

Kiernan held his breath.

"I said yes. I love him very much."

He didn't quite know what to say. He was stunned, in a way, that life moved on. Stunned that he had missed the developing relationship between Adele and Mark. Stunned at his sister's ability to say yes to love all over again.

"Congratulations," he said gruffly. He realized he was shaken but glad for her. "I guess maybe you did get the miracle you were looking for. But don't get any ideas about me."

"I have been looking for a miracle for you," she said, "but I was looking in one direction, and it came from another."

"There have been no miracles here," he warned her. "None."

"Hmm."

"Don't say hmm, like that. If you think that lying little chit of an imposter nanny is a miracle, you need a little miracle research."

"I did some research, you know. On her. That's why I acted as if I knew her when I got here. I kind of did. You can find out the most amazing things on the internet."

He really wanted to pretend he was not interested in this. He wanted his sister to think he was completely indifferent to what she had discovered about Stacy Walker Murphy on the internet.

Instead, in a voice he hoped was stripped of anything that could be interpreted as interest, Kiernan heard himself say, "Like?"

CHAPTER THIRTEEN

"Her whole family was killed in a car accident when she was sixteen," Adele told him, her voice aching with tenderness.

"I know that already."

"Oh." Adele cocked her head at him. "Did you look her up on the internet, too?"

"No."

"So, she told you that?"

"To try and wangle her way by my defenses!"

"She *has* used her greatest tragedy as a tool, but, as shocking as this will be to you, it doesn't have anything to do with you. She started that group."

"Career and College Opportunities for Orphans."

"Foster kids," his sister corrected him mildly. She twirled some hair around her little finger. "She told you that, too?"

"She mentioned it briefly."

"Ah. You seemed to have known each other quite a short time to have shared so deeply."

He glared at Adele. "I *regret* that. I don't see it as cause for celebration. Look, the facts are the facts. She misrepresented herself on purpose. She's a writer not a nanny."

"She's a good one, too. I read some of her stuff online. She would be a great person to entrust your story to."

"What story?" he asked dangerously. "Look, sis, she needs to go. She does not need to be adopted by you."

"She's always dreamed of a winter holiday," Adele said with a frightening softness, not hearing the danger in his voice at all. "She's had so much go wrong in her life. She expects the worst."

Poster child for Murphy's Law he remembered her introducing herself.

"And I can hardly blame her. There's a video online—" She stopped.

"A video? Of Stacy?"

"I cannot believe you didn't go online yourself when you found out she wasn't a nanny!"

"Well, I didn't. What's the video of?"

"Never mind. It's not important. What's important is that she's worked really hard at giving things to others. I looked up that charity online. For a group with very little money and a low profile, they accomplish quite a bit. They've handed out two dozen scholarships in the past eight years."

"Earth-shattering," he said drily.

"That's twenty-four young people changed forever. For your information, that *is* earth-shattering."

"Okay, so the company will donate some money," he said.

His sister gave him a look that said he was missing the point.

"And provide some people with know-how to get her little group off the ground."

"You're missing the point."

"Which is?"

"She expects the worst."

"It's her karma," he growled. "What do you expect with a middle name like Murphy?"

"Do not hide behind flippancy with me," his sister warned. He really hated it when she took that tone.

But then her voice softened, "What if the best thing ever happened to her? What if good came from this predicament she finds herself in, instead of bad?"

"What would she learn from that?"

"That life is good!"

"Well, it isn't!" But, he thought, though the thought was unwilling as hell, it had been good. It had been unexpectedly good for a few short days with Stacy. Not that he could ever let Adele know that!

His sister looked at him, then shook her head with disappointment. He felt her disappointment in him all the way to his toes.

He had been Adele's hero since they were kids.

Not that he deserved that title now!

"When did you become *this* person?" Adele asked.

"I'm protecting myself."

"Against what?"

"Against life, as if you should have to ask. I became *this* person the day that Danner died."

His sister suddenly looked very, very angry.

"No one," she said, her words angry, "would hate that more than him. That you would make that his legacy to the world is disgraceful. He embraced life. He treated it all like an incredible adventure, and I'm grateful for that. I'm grateful for the person I am because I got to be with him for a short time. I'm grateful for my son."

Kiernan remembered Stacy, too, had made gratitude her legacy from tragedy.

"For God's sake," his sister said, "that girl has lost everything. You are in a position to get out of your big, fat self-pitying self and do something for her."

His big, fat, self-pitying self?

"She lied to me!"

"If you couldn't tell who Stacy Walker was from the minute you laid eyes on her, there is no hope for you, Kiernan McAllister. None at all."

He remembered claiming Stacy's lips earlier.

And knowing, just as his sister had said, the absolute truth about her.

And of course, the danger she posed to him on many levels.

His sister shot him one last meaningful look and flounced off the bed, tossing her hair. She marched from his room, closing his door with a snap behind her.

One of the things that was not good about being very powerful was that people stopped telling you the truth and started telling you what you wanted to hear. One of the people he could trust not to do that was Adele.

Kiernan recognized that this brief encounter with Stacy had rocked his world, that he could not think with his normal discernment and detachment. His sister was trying to steer him in the right direction.

And his sister had never come from any place but love.

He told himself he was not going to look on his computer. He lasted about thirty seconds before he went and retrieved it from his dresser. Sometimes the internet worked up here and mostly it didn't. He was hoping it wouldn't, but he typed in her name anyway.

A video called *Proposal Fail* came up.

Stacy looked gorgeous: her hair and makeup done, in a sexy dress and high heels. He recognized the restaurant as one of Vancouver's best.

But, despite how gorgeous she looked and the fact she was in one of Vancouver's most upscale restaurants, the scene had obviously been captured after she was already angry.

"You want me to what?" she asked, her voice high and shrill.

The guy looked around nervously, twirled his wineglass and wouldn't look at her.

Kiernan found himself looking at the beau critically. She would take *him* back?

Dylan had guffawed when she had said that, apparently more loudly than she had thought.

"I thought you were going to ask me to marry you, and you're asking me to shack up with you?"

"Shack up, Stacy, really? What century is that from?"

Kiernan had the ugly feeling if he could, he would have crawled through the computer screen, picked that guy up by his throat and knocked his teeth out.

He had obviously caused Stacy intense pain… and instead of trying to make it better, he had a sneering look on his face.

She'd go back to him? Really?

Kiernan watched Stacy stand up. Pick up her wine. Take a fortifying sip and then walk over to her beau.

She dumped the whole glass over his head. It was red and it stained his pristine white shirt beyond repair.

"What century is that from?" she yelled for the entertainment of the whole world.

Only Kiernan didn't feel entertained at all. He could clearly see she was crying as she stormed from the room. The guy looked more annoyed about his shirt than the fact his girlfriend had just left him.

Good grief, what kind of bad luck was it to have a moment like that posted?

He had a moment of clarity as he shut off his computer.

What if it wasn't all about him? Adele was so right. Despite a life threaded through with the worst kind of tragedy, Stacy was struggling valiantly to make it a better place. Even while she claimed her own dreams were in tatters, he knew she really stood on the edge.

Of going to the place where he was, a place of hopelessness and cynicism that he would not wish on anyone, or a place of being returned to faith.

He seemed like the last person who could be

entrusted with an assignment like that—a return to faith—but really, it would not take much of a push to get her moving in the right direction.

What if he could, in some small way, get out of his big, fat, self-pitying self to help another human being to believe in dreams again?

His sister, he was pretty sure, was entirely correct about him. There was no hope for him. None at all.

But despite her denials, he had seen in Stacy's face she clung to hope the way a person who had survived a shipwreck clung to the lifeboat.

There was no sense crushing that thing called hope simply because he could not feel it!

What if he could do some small thing that would change her? Give her a much-needed boost? Not just protect her from the return of her boyfriend or a life as a crazy cat lady, but help her believe in the power of her dreams all over again?

He went down the hall to the room his sister preferred. She had moved Max's playpen in there and was sitting on the bed, leafing through a book.

"What would you suggest?" he asked his sister.

She looked up from the book. A light came on in her face. That light almost made the chance he was taking worth it. Of course, he thought she was going to suggest something he could *buy.* An all-expense-paid week or two to a world-class resort. Like Whistler, only that was probably too close to home to seem like a real dream.

Steamboat, Colorado, maybe.

Les Trois Vallées, in the French Alps. Why had he thought of that? Because of Brides-les-Bains, one of those three very famous resorts?

If his mind was making weird jumps in logic like that: from helping her dreams come true to thinking of her in any context with *bride* in it, then the farther away the better.

"I was thinking you should take her up to Last Chance tomorrow," his sister said.

He had to refuse. Last Chance was, in his opinion, one of the most beautiful places on the planet. And Kiernan had been to many beautiful places on the planet.

The humble little cabin named Last Chance, behind his house, way up the mountain in a grove of old, old cedar, as well as having one of the most panoramic views he had ever seen, had its own private natural hot spring.

"Can you think of a better place for the perfect winter getaway?" Adele asked.

No, he couldn't. On the other hand, did he really want to be at a place named Last Chance with Stacy Walker? Last chance to make things right? To be a better man?

Last chance to hope, to live again, to...

As well as being remote and beautiful, it was a place of romance and magic.

"I'll come, too," Adele said, as if she read each of his doubts. "We can put Max in the sled and you can pull it."

The truth? He'd always had trouble saying no to his sister. Since he had killed her husband, the father of her child, his sense of obligation to her, of somehow wanting to make up to her that which could never be made up felt like a boulder sitting on his chest, slowly crushing the life out of him.

He owed his sister big-time, a debt he had no hope of repaying. There was that word again, hope.

And so if Adele wanted to take Stacy Murphy Walker to Last Chance, that was what he would help her do. He was being given an opportunity to get out of his big, fat, self-pitying self long enough to be the better man.

Temporarily.

CHAPTER FOURTEEN

"LAST CHANCE?" STACY said, dubiously. "What is that?"

Kiernan glared at her. She was looking the proverbial gift horse in the mouth. He was doing her a favor. He was making her dreams come true, for Pete's sake. Did she have to look so reluctant? But things had been awkward between them since he had kissed her.

That kiss in the kitchen was supposed to have been *goodbye*. But she was still here, and the memory of that kiss sizzled in the air between them this morning.

"It's actually the reason I bought this property," he said, striving for patience in the face of her lack of enthusiasm. "Danner found this little cabin to rent one winter. The only way you can reach it once the snow flies is on cross-country skis. There's a natural hot spring right beside it."

He could see the war in her face.

"Perfect winter getaway," he said. "I've been at some of the best resorts in the world, and it beats all of them. And it's a two-hour ski from here."

He'd almost had her, until he'd mentioned the ski part.

"Oh, I've never skied. I'm sure I would make a complete fool of myself. No, really, now that your sister is here, I have to leave."

Her voice was firm, but unless he missed his guess, Stacy looked wistful. Besides, when he saw her fear of making a fool of herself, he thought of that internet video posting, knew she was still suffering the humiliation of it and committed even more to convincing her to go. He hated the thought of her going through life being afraid to do things.

"The roads are worse this morning than they were last night," Kiernan said. Well, since the fear was there anyway, he might as well press it to his advantage. He hoped her fear of driving on the roads would be greater than her fear of making a fool of herself.

"And I still don't think the snow will last," he continued. "This might be your only opportunity to get up there."

"Last chance?" she said, and hazarded a smile.

"Exactly."

He certainly wasn't inviting her back here, ever.

Because she did all sorts of things to him that he wasn't sure he wanted done. Like made him aware, for the first time in a long time, what it felt like to be alive.

To notice what the light looked like kissing chocolate curls and how her laughter, ringing out with the baby's laughter, made everything different.

Who was he kidding?

The moment the shift had happened was when his lips touched hers.

"I don't have any of the right stuff," she said, and now he could hear in her voice, too, that she had capitulated and was wistful to go.

"Don't worry, I have all the right stuff."

And she looked at him as if that could be taken two ways and that maybe she really thought he did have all the right stuff, despite the fact he had been a complete jerk to her.

Well, she had been frantic in her attempts to make amends. He had slept aware it was her hands that had put the sheets on his bed, with a belly satisfyingly full of really good things.

So, he would make amends, too.

Give her that winter holiday she had always wanted, then send her on her way. No more kissing. *Toodle-oo.*

Kieran McAllister frowned. He did not say *toodle-oo.* Maybe one more kiss to cement it in her mind about leaving both cats and the old boyfriend out of her plans for the future.

The thought of that kiss may have flashed through his eyes, because she looked flustered suddenly, too.

He wasn't going to kiss her again. "We're going to be chaperoned!" he recalled, a touch desperately. "Adele and Ivan are coming, too."

"Oh!" Stacy still seemed underenthused.

And he recognized he had to take a risk. He had to tell her the truth.

"And I've behaved badly toward you," he said. "I don't want our time together to end on this note."

And instantly he was aware of the most dangerous thing of all: this really wasn't about her, no matter how he tried to cloak it in altruism.

He did not want their time together to end at all.

Was that why he was really offering her the journey to Last Chance? It was. It was to see if there was any hope at all, and if there was, if he was brave enough to reach for it, to reach for the life rope that had been thrown into the quagmire he had existed in.

The truth was he needed this trip to Last Chance way more than she did.

Something softened in her face, and he knew she had heard the truth. And he knew she was remembering: snowmen and snow angels and dodging popcorn missiles and sharing ordinary moments together that had somehow become extraordinary.

"Yes, all right," Stacy said. "I'd like that."

Thank goodness for chaperones, he thought.

But Adele announced, minutes before they were set to leave, that she wasn't coming. Stacy reacted to the announcement by blushing, Kiernan smelled a rat, the same as he had when Max had been left in his office without warning.

"I think Max is getting a cold," Adele said. "It wouldn't be good for him to be outside all day. Look at his nose."

Kiernan, to his everlasting regret, looked at his nephew's nose. Even his sister could not manufacture something like that!

In light of Stacy's blush of discomfort, he debated canceling. But only for about two seconds.

Because sometime during the night he realized he was looking forward to going up there as much as he had looked forward to anything for a long, long time.

And he knew part of it was he was excited about showing it to her, the nanny imposter.

How could he think that—nanny imposter—and feel only amusement and no anger at all?

He was working at being a better man. He would show her a great day, enjoy her wonder, bring her home.

There would be absolutely no need to reinforce the cat, ex-boyfriend lesson.

With his lips!

Stacy probably needed her head examined, but here she was having a ski lesson from Kieran McAllister

She hadn't even backed out when she heard Adele and Max were not coming.

Because, really, she had played it safe her entire life. And where had that gotten her?

No, if she had learned one thing in her short time here, it was this: when things started spinning out of control, go with it rather than fight it!

And spinning out of control was a very apt description of how she had felt after Kiernan had kissed her in the kitchen.

One kiss, and she was pretty sure she was cured forever of wanting Dylan back. Or a cat.

Though as a point of pride, she could not let Kiernan know that his kiss had cured her of those desires.

What she did desire now, in a way she had never wanted it before, was to embrace it all, including the uncertainty she felt every single time she looked at Kiernan.

She was being offered an adventure. Not just any adventure. A chance to do something she had longed to do ever since she had enjoyed the snow with her beloved father.

Her dad had never called her Stacy. He had always, affectionately, teasingly called her Murphy.

Bur for once something seemed to be going right for her, and she was not saying no to that.

And it was true she was getting in way over her head with this family. Since Kiernan had kissed her, she felt as if she had the shivers, which could not be cured by anything, not even a roaring fire in the hearth in the great room.

But the thing was, she didn't mind feeling that way.

She felt alive. And so, marveling at the unexpected spin her life had taken, she watched Kiernan get ready.

His comfort with the equipment inspired confidence. She watched him waxing the skis, listened to him explaining how the waxes depended on the temperature and the snow.

"You can buy skis that don't need waxing, but I don't," he said. "I'm a purist."

There was a whole section underneath the back deck of his house devoted to outdoor equipment. He could provide skis and snowshoes and skates to about twenty people.

"We always make a skating rink at the back of the house later in the year," he told her.

And Stacy's desire shifted again: to see that. To see him on skates, to have him teach her that, too. But she knew that was taking it too far into the future, and that today was called the present, because that's what it was, a gift.

A gift that did not promise the future.

She vowed to herself she would just enjoy this day without overlaying it with anxiety about what could possibly happen next.

He'd had no trouble at all finding her size of skis and boots. Adele had lent her a jacket that fit, a hat and good mittens.

"Are we getting on a chairlift?" she asked nervously, despite her confidence in him, she had some doubts about herself. *Anything that can go wrong, will.*

He laughed. "No lifts for this. This is cross-country skiing," he said. "It's way different than downhill skiing, which is the chairlift kind."

"In what way is it different?"

"More work. Everything we do, we do under our own power." Satisfied with the wax, he led the way outside and set two pairs of skis on the ground.

"Okay, these are yours. Put your toe in there and step down."

It was difficult to hold one foot up, position it into a very small area and step down. Her foot slid uncooperatively everywhere *but* into the binding.

To her embarrassment, he had to get down in the snow and guide her foot into the right place, snap the binding down. Then, while he was already on the ground, he did the other one, too.

She looked down at his head. That their acquaintance could be marked in days seemed impossible.

She felt as if she had known Kiernan McAllister forever.

And would know him forever.

And there went her vow not to spoil any part of this day fretting about the future and what could happen next.

Still, it took all her will to stop herself from reaching out and sliding her hand through the silk of his hair. He glanced up at her, his long lashes over those amazing silver eyes holding speckles of frost. Her heart swooped upward, like a bird that had been freed from a cage.

Was she falling in love with him?

Of course not. She reprimanded herself. She barely knew him.

But she *had* kissed him. And made a snowman

with him. And lain on her back beside him, their cold hands intertwined as they looked at the stars and exchanged confidences.

Of course she did not love him. But the air seemed to sparkle with diamond drops of possibility that outshone the diamond drops that sparkled in the pristine snow all around them.

She felt some exquisite awareness tickling along her spine as she watched him expertly step into his skis.

And then, thankfully, the time for thinking was done, because she was swept into a world of movement and laughter, pure physical activity and exertion.

"I'll show you a few basic moves." He showed her the step and glide.

Then she tried it. "Argh! You are pure power and grace. I am a penguin waddling!"

"Relax. It's all just for fun. I'll break trail, you put your skis in my tracks and follow me. Just do what I do and everything will be fine."

And then, amazingly she did relax, because he was in front of her and not witnessing her clumsy efforts to follow his ski tracks. It was fun and easier than she had anticipated.

"See? Everything is fine, isn't it?"

And it was. No, it was more than fine. Seconds from the house, they entered the trees. The silence was broken only by the occasional branch letting go of its load of snow, and her breathing, loud in her own ears.

"You doing okay?" he called.

"It is hard work. But so much fun!"

He glanced over his shoulder at her, his approving smile lit up her world.

She loved being behind him. She could drink her fill of him without him ever knowing how she gloried in his easy strength, his power, his confidence.

The woods were extraordinarily silent and beautiful. They had been making their way up a very gradual slope, and now it steepened.

"Like this," he said. He set his skis like triangles and walked his way up the hill, making a fishbone pattern in the new snow. She tried it. Now this was harder than he had made it look.

Partway up the incline, she could feel herself sliding back instead of going forward. She let out a little shriek of dismay, threw herself forward on her poles and froze leaning heavily on them.

He looked back at her and burst out laughing. He turned and skied back to her, stopping with a swish of snow.

"I'm stuck," she said.

"I can see that," he said with a smile. "I'll get you unstuck."

He regarded her predicament thoughtfully, then pulled in right behind her, his skis forming a sandwich around her own.

She could feel his breath on her neck, and his hands went to the small of her back and he shoved.

"Okay," he said, his breath still warm on her neck and tickling her ears, "pull with your poles and dig in those edges. That's it. Just one small step. Good. And another one."

A lot of things seemed to be coming unstuck, most of them within her.

"I'm sliding back on your skis." She was. She slid right back into him, and for a breathless moment they stood there, glued together, the majesty of the quiet mountains all around them.

His arms folded lightly around her. "You're doing great." And then he let her go and shoved her again.

Huffing and puffing, she managed to inch her way up the steep incline.

"You've got it." And then he left his place behind her and moved ahead of her, with a powerful skating motion that broke the trail.

Of course, what goes up must come down, and as she crested the hill, she saw it was a long downhill run.

He swooped down it, a cry of pure joy coming off his lips. She watched as he invited speed, crouched, played with the hill and the snow and gravity.

He reached the bottom, slid to a sideways stop in an incredible display of agility and spray of snow.

"Come on," he called.

The truth was she was terrified. Her heart was doing that beating-too-fast thing that it had been doing for almost two full days. She stared down the hill. It seemed a long way down. And it seemed very steep.

"You can sidestep it if you want," he called. He climbed partway back up the hill and demonstrated a way she could come down.

But suddenly she didn't want to play it safe.

She let out a war whoop and shoved her poles to get going. Then she was swooshing down the hill so fast she could feel her stomach drop. Her eyes got tears in them. Her hat flew off.

She gained speed. She let out another whoop, the pure joy of letting go completely! She raced by him, screaming with laughter.

Except that beyond him, he had not broken the trail. Her skis hit the virgin snow and slowed so abruptly she thought she was going to be tossed right out of her bindings.

As soon as she started to think about what could happen, it did. She caught an edge and could feel herself cartwheeling through the snow.

Only it didn't hurt. It was like tumbling into a cold pillow. After she stopped, she lay there for a moment, staring at the sky.

He skied over and peered down at her. "Are you okay?" he asked.

"Really?" she said. "Never better."

And then they were both laughing.

And it felt as if *really* she had never had a better moment in her whole life.

CHAPTER FIFTEEN

TWO HOURS LATER, coated in generous amounts of sweat, crusted in snow and dazzled by laughter and the sun that had come out on the mountain, they burst into a small clearing.

Stacy was aware that Kiernan was watching her, and from the small smile that played across his lips, her reaction did not disappoint.

She clapped her wet, mittened hands over her mouth, but not before a gasp of pure wonder escaped it.

There was a cabin at the far edge of the clearing. It was tiny and humble, the logs long since weathered to gray. And yet, set amongst the drifts of snow, with snow sparkling on its roof and the red curtains showing through the window, it was a homey sight in the middle of the majesty of the mountains. Even the little outhouse that was behind it, a half-moon carved in the door, was adorable.

On the other side of the cabin, a stream trickled down rocks, heavy mist rising off of it.

"What is that smell?" she asked, the only thing not in keeping with the beauty of the scene.

"That stream is a natural hot spring. You're smelling minerals, mostly sulfur. Despite the smell, they are supposed to be very good for you. Tracks show us that even the animals come here. Come on. I'll show you."

He glided forward. After two hours, she felt her abilities had not improved all that much. She still waddled after him.

He skied right to the cabin, kicked off his skis and shrugged off the pack he had carried the entire way. She arrived and he showed her how to release the binding by putting the tip of the pole on it and pushing.

She stepped out of the skis and had to reach for his arm.

"My legs feel wobbly," she said, and then let go of his arm and went to the edge of the water.

"That water will have you feeling back to normal in no time." He had come to stand beside her.

"This must have taken someone hundreds of

painstaking hours," she said, regarding the rock pool, complete with an underwater bench that had been built to capture the steaming water from the springs.

"I had the good fortune to get it exactly as it was. You see how the water is seeping out of the rocks on the downhill side? It acts as a natural filtration system. The water is constantly being replaced."

"The rocks are like artwork," she said. The constant flow of water over them turned colors that might have been muted if they were dry to spectacularly jewel like. There were rocks in golds and greens and grays and blues and pinks.

"Are we going to go in that?" she breathed.

"Of course. If you brought a bathing suit."

Her face crumpled. "No. You never said to. I'm not sure I would have believed you if you had. This is pure magic, Kieran, but I didn't bring a suit. I guess I can't go in."

He raised an eyebrow wickedly. "Unless..."

"No!" she said.

"Well, guess what, Murphy?"

"What?"

"Unless somebody has figured out that anything that can go wrong will, and that someone had your back."

Him?

She could feel tears pricking her eyes.

"What's the matter?" he asked softly.

"Nothing. My dad used to call me Murphy. No one has for a long time."

"Ah, Murphy," he said gruffly, put his arm around her shoulders and pulled her hard against his own shoulder. "Adele packed you a bathing suit," he said, his tone gentle as a touch.

"Oh, Adele," she said, not sure if she was disappointed or relieved. Well, maybe relieved. She certainly wouldn't want him packing her a bathing suit. Come to that, did she want to be sharing a very romantic moment with him in a bathing suit she had not even chosen herself?

"She packed us lunch, too. You want to do that first?"

She realized she was ravenous…and that lunch would give her reprieve from donning the bathing suit. It was hard enough to put on a bathing suit you had chosen yourself, after many self-critical moments in front of the mirror. What would Adele have chosen for her?

He laughed at her expression. "Lunch it is. We just burned about a million calories each." He opened the backpack and took out the contents. "Hot dogs and marshmallows. A good thing we burned so many calories."

He rummaged through the pack some more. "Look, she packed a bottle of wine to go with our hot dogs." He shook his head. "Not exactly hot dog wine. It's a rare bottle of ice wine."

"We don't have to drink it," Stacy said. In fact probably better if they did not. "You are probably saving that for a special occasion."

"I was," he said, rummaging again, and then he hesitated at something he found in that pack, "and I can't think of an occasion more special than this one."

"In what way?" she stammered.

"Part of the snow virgin ceremonies," he teased, and pulled something else out of the pack and held it up.

"I'm pretty sure I lost my snow virginity on the night of the snowball fight," she choked out. "Snowball fight. Snow angel. Snowman. Yup. Done."

"I'm pretty sure you're not done until you've been dipped in the waters of Last Chance in this."

She looked at the tiny piece of black-and-white fabric he was waving, not comprehending.

"Adele packed you a bikini!"

Well, that answered the burning question of what kind of bathing suit Adele had packed for her!

"Let's eat," she said, strangled.

"How are you at fire starting?"

"Is this still part of the whole snow virgin thing? Because I'd be about the same at that as I am at snowman building. And skiing."

"All the same," he said, and tossed a package of matches at her. "You can be in charge of the fire pit out here. I'm going to start a fire in stove in the cabin, too, so we have a warm place to get changed."

Into a black-and-white bikini that looked, at a glance, as if it didn't have enough fabric in it to make a good-size handkerchief.

She was probably going to need the wine to find the nerve to put on the bathing suit. Meanwhile, she would distract herself by trying to start a fire.

Kiernan came back outside and helped her. Soon he had turned her little pile of twigs and tiny flame into a roaring blaze and they were toasting hot dogs on sticks over it.

"Oh, my," she said an hour later. "Did I eat three hot dogs?"

"You did."

"Why did it taste like food from the gods?"

"They're pleased about the sacrificing of the snow virgin?" He laughed at her face. It was so good to hear him laugh like that, boyishly, carelessly, mischievously. He could tease her for a hundred years about being a snow virgin, if she just got to hear him laugh.

"I'm getting a little confused," she said. "Am I being sacrificed or deflowered?"

It was her turn to feel richly satisfied when a tide of brick-red worked its way up the strong column of his neck.

"The cabin is probably warm by now, if you want to go put on your suit," he said gruffly, not looking at her. Really, for the first time since she had gotten on those skies, it felt as if she had the upper hand.

The inside of the cabin was rudimentary but

darling. She found the bathing suit wrapped in a towel on the bed.

It was definitely the tiniest bathing suit she had ever put on! So much for having the upper hand. Stacy felt like a nervous wreck after donning the bathing suit. There wasn't even a mirror to check how revealing it was. She wrapped herself in a towel and headed outside.

He was already in the hot pool and she gulped at the pure wonder of the moment life had delivered.

She slipped off the towel and felt a surge of fresh wonder at the look in his eyes, stormy with appreciation, on her. Rough stone steps went into the water, and she took them and then waded across to the bench on the opposite side of the pool from him.

After a moment, she closed her eyes and allowed herself to feel the full glory of it: the hot, natural water massaging her exhausted muscles and her many bruises.

"I didn't really realize I hurt all over, until I got in here," she said.

"You took some pretty good tumbles."

"The water feels great on all my aches and

pains. I didn't deserve a day like this, Kiernan. Does it mean you have forgiven me?"

She opened her eyes and looked at him. She saw his answer before he said it.

"Yeah," he said, "I suppose that is what it means."

"Thank you." She took a deep breath. "Now you just have to forgive yourself."

He looked across the steam at her, raised an eyebrow. "What do you mean by that, exactly?"

"Your sister and I talked last night."

"That was my fear," he said.

"She's fallen in love."

"Yes, she told me."

"She's worried about you accepting Mark. She's worried you can't get beyond what happened that day."

"Are you giving me some free counseling?" he said.

She could hear the warning in his voice, to back off, to leave it, but she could not.

"Why are you mad at Mark?"

"I'm not mad at him."

"Adele said you seem furious with him. She thinks it's because he lived and Danner died."

Kiernan swore softly. "That's not it. That's not it at all!"

"What is it then?"

"It's that I lived and Danner died."

"And Mark?"

"He was there." The anger faded from him, and he looked dejected. She saw his heart, and it was just as she had always suspected. She saw Kiernan McAllister's heart and it was broken.

She scooted over on the bench beside him and took his hand. "He was there and...?" she whispered.

"He was there for the moment of my greatest failing," Kiernan said. "It's not his fault, but I can barely look at him. Because he knows."

"Knows what?"

Kiernan's sigh was long and followed by a shudder so massive that the water of the pool rippled.

"It was my fault. I killed him."

She was silent, but her hand tightened on his, and her eyes would not leave his face.

"Danner was different than me. I had used adrenaline all my life, like a drug. Flying down a mountain, flat out, there is nothing else. Just that moment."

"I just experienced that myself," Stacy said.

He nodded. "Danner was more like you. Willing to embrace it, but cautious. I introduced him to that world of untouched snow, but he never took leadership. He always trusted me and followed me.

"And that morning, I picked the wrong slope. And I was strong enough and experienced enough to outrun it, and he was not."

He stopped, but she had read it in his voice and his eyes and the heave of his shoulders.

"And I will feel guilty about that for the rest of my life. That I misjudged his ability to cope and it cost him his life. I will feel responsible for that for the rest of my life.

"When I close my eyes, I can still see it and feel it. I glanced back over my shoulder, could see his skies cutting a line out, setting a shelf of snow free. The sound was like a freight train. It was right on top of both of us. I was closer to Mark, and I shoved him hard, and he saw what was going on and managed to kind of squirt out to the side.

"I thought Danner was right on my shoulder. I could feel the wind being created by that snow coming. But when I skied free of it, he wasn't there. He'd been swept away."

The silence of the mountains felt heavy and sacred.

"But what could you have done differently?" she finally whispered.

"That is what I lay awake at night asking myself. That's why I wish sometimes it would have taken me, too. So that I would not have to live with this ultimate failure, the sense of being powerless when it mattered most. The only time it really ever mattered."

"And Adele would have lost both of you, maybe even all three of you," Stacy said softly. "I don't know that she could have survived that."

"What if we'd had breakfast a little later, or decided not to go out that day, or what if I had asked to take a different trail?"

"That's why it's your fault?" she asked quietly.

"It's part of it. Wrong decisions, from the very beginning of that day." His voice was broken.

"My family dying was my fault, too," she whispered.

His head jerked up.

"I was going to my first high school dance. Oh, Kiernan, I was so excited. I had a new dress, and I'd been allowed to wear makeup, and my mom had done my hair for me. My imagination, of course," she admitted ruefully, "had gone absolutely crazy creating scenarios. I thought Bobby Brighton might notice me and ask me to dance. Or Kenny O'Connell.

"And then I got there, and it wasn't like the middle school dances, where everybody just kind of danced together, and had fun.

"All the boys were on one side of the room, and all the girls on the other, and pretty soon all the popular girls were being asked to dance, and I wasn't. By the halfway intermission, I hadn't been asked to dance, not even once, not even by the science nerds.

"And so I called my Dad. And I was crying.

"And he said my grandma was over visiting, and they had been talking about going out bowling and for iced hot chocolate after, *and Murphy, girl, we wouldn't have had any fun without you, anyway, so I'm coming to get you. And when I*

*get there, I better not be beating off those boys
with my shovel.*

"But—" Her voice had become a whisper.
"They never got there. A drunk driver ran a red
light and it killed them all."

"Stacy," he said, and his voice was a whisper
that shared her agony.

"I didn't tell you that because I wanted you to
feel sorry for me," she said. "I told you because I
always felt I had killed them, too. If I hadn't have
called. Was my Dad rushing to get to me? Was
he so focused on the fact his little Murphy girl
was in distress, he missed something, that flash
of motion, or a sound that would have alerted
him to the fact that car was coming? I have tor-
mented myself with this question—what if I had
called ten minutes later or earlier?"

"Stacy," he said again, and now his powerful
arms were wrapped around her, and he pulled
her hard against himself.

"Do you think I killed them?" she demanded.

"No! Of course not!"

"I don't think you killed Danner, either."

Beneath his skin, for a moment she thought she
felt his heart stop beating. And then it started

again and instead of putting her away from him, he drew her closer.

He pushed the tendrils of wet hair from her face, and he looked down at her, and it felt as if no one had ever seen her quite so completely before.

"Thank you," he whispered.

And it was a greater gift, even, than being brought to this incredible place.

CHAPTER SIXTEEN

KIERNAN WAITED FOR it to happen. All his strength had not been enough to hold the lid on the place that contained the grief within him.

The touch of her hand, the look in her eyes, and his strength had abandoned him, and he had told her all of it: his failure and his powerlessness.

Now, sitting beside her, her hand in his, the wetness of her hair resting on his shoulder, he waited for everything to fade: the white-topped mountains that surrounded him, the feel of the hot water against his skin, the way her hand felt in his.

He waited for all that to fade, and for the darkness to take its place, to ooze through him like thick, black sludge freed from a containment pond, blotting out all else.

Instead, astounded, Kiernan became *more* aware of everything around him, as if he was soaking up life through his pores, breathing in glory through his nose, becoming drenched in light instead of darkness.

He started to laugh.

"What?" she asked, a smile playing across the lovely fullness of her lips.

"I just feel alive. For the past few days, I have felt alive. And I don't know if that's a good thing or a bad thing."

"This is what I think," she said, slowly and thoughtfully, "we are, all of us, vulnerable to love. And when we lose someone, or something that we have cared about, we are like Samson. We think the source of our strength is gone. We have had our hair cut.

"But without our even realizing it, our hair grows back, and our strength returns, and maybe," she finished softly, "just maybe we are even better than we were before."

Her words fell on him, like raindrops hitting a desert that was too long parched.

His awareness shifted to her, and being with her seemed to fill him to overflowing.

He dropped his head over hers and took her lips. He kissed her with warmth and with welcome, a man who had thought he was dead discovering not just that he lived but, astonishingly, that he wanted to live.

Stacy returned his kiss, her lips parting under his, her hands twining around his neck, pulling him in even closer to her.

There was gentle welcome. She had seen all of him, he had bared his weakness and his darkness to her, and still he felt only acceptance from her.

But acceptance was slowly giving way to something else. There was hunger in her, and he sensed an almost savage need in her to go to the place a kiss like this took a man and a woman.

With great reluctance he broke the kiss, cupped her cheeks in his hands and looked down at her.

He felt as if he was memorizing each of her features: the green of those amazing eyes, her dark brown hair curling even more wildly from the steam of the hot spring, the swollen plumpness of her lips, the whiteness of her skin.

"It's too soon for this," he said, his voice hoarse.

"I know," she said, and her voice was raw, too.

And then, despite having said that, they were drawn together again, into that sensual world of steam and hot water, skin like warmed-through silk touching skin. Peripherally, he was aware of snow shining with diamonds, and mountain peaks soaring to touch sky, and the insistent call of a Whiskey Jack.

He pulled away from her the second time.

It was too soon to kiss her so thoroughly. Their days together had been intense. This feeling of being cracked wide open was something that could make a man do something irrational.

And he could not do that to her. You did not kiss a woman like Stacy Murphy Walker like that unless you knew.

Unless you knew what your feelings were.

And unless you knew the future held some possibility.

He had brought her here as a gift, to help her heal her pain, not to cause her more. But he had come here for himself, too. Maybe mostly for himself. To see if there was hope, and it seemed to him that maybe there was, after all.

And it seemed to him part of hoping, part of breaking open inside was a requirement to have the events of his life to make him better.

Not bitter.

Worthy of the love of a beautiful woman like this one.

That's what Adele had tried to tell him. That's what Danner would have wanted. Danner would have wanted him to embrace *all* of what he was, darkness and light, and let them melt together.

"We need to go," he said, letting go of Stacy reluctantly, knowing he could not push the bounds of his own strength by kissing her a third time.

He stood up, put his hands on the rock edges of the pool and heaved himself out of it. "We don't want to be trying to get home in the dark."

It was an excuse. An excuse to step back from the intensity between them. Because that kind of intensity did not lend itself to rational thought and it seemed to him he owed her at least that.

To make decisions from here on out, as far as she was concerned, based on reason.

And not what he had felt there in the pool with her: the powerful release of something he had been holding on to, followed all too quickly by the ecstasy of her lips on his.

She looked disappointed.

And maybe a touch relieved, too, as if she knew things were going too fast, spinning out of their control.

He grabbed his dry clothes from the toasty

warm cabin, leaving it to her to get dressed in privacy. He ducked behind the cabin, hoping the cold air on his heated skin would be sobering.

Instead, being able to feel the cold air prickle across his skin only increased his sense of being alive as totally and completely as he ever had been. He quickly packed up their things, waited for her to come out of the cabin and resisted the temptation to greet her with a kiss, as if they had been separated by weeks instead of minutes.

He schooled himself to be all business as he helped her into her skis. The sun was now warm, and the snow was melting quickly. It made it heavy and hard to ski, despite the fact he had changed waxes. Partway home, they lost the snow completely.

They took off the skis, and he shouldered them. They walked along the forest trail. Stacy slipped at one point, and he reached back and took her hand, and somehow he didn't let it go again until he noticed she was limping.

"Are you okay?"

"I think the ski boots are rubbing."

"Let's have a look."

"It's okay. I can practically see your house from here."

"I think I should have a look."

Cross-country boots were not made for walking. His were custom, so they fit him well, but hers were not.

They sat in the snow, and he took her boots off, and then her socks. She did, indeed, have terrible rubs starting on the back of both heels. One of them was bleeding.

"Why didn't you say something sooner?"

She looked sheepish. "To tell you the truth, I hardly noticed."

And so, she, like him, was in an altered state, one where maybe the best decisions were not made.

With a tenderness he had not known he was capable of, he found a little of the snow that remained in a shaded spot beside the trail and rubbed it on the frayed skin of her heels, aware of how he loved caressing her feet and the look on her face when he did it.

And then, ignoring her protests, feeling stronger than he had ever felt, feeling like Samson who once again had hair, he picked her up and cradled her against his chest.

"I can walk," she protested.

But he didn't want her to. He wanted to carry her. He wanted to protect her and care for her. Maybe he wanted to show her how strong he was.

"What about the skis?" she asked, when it was evident he did not intend to put her down.

"I'll get you there and then I'll come back for them."

She looked as if she was going to protest. But then she didn't. She snuggled deep into his chest, and he strode along the trail that led toward home.

He set her down on the front steps of his house, and still feeling strong and full of energy, he went back up the trail to retrieve their skis.

When he came back to the house, she was waiting at the door. He could tell by the look on her face something was wrong.

"What is it?"

She passed him the note. In Adele's handwriting it said that Max had gotten worse since they left and had developed a high fever. She had taken him to the hospital in Whistler.

Kiernan stared at the note.

It seemed as if his whole world crashed in around him. While he'd been out playing in the snow, entertaining foolish notions about the nature of love and forever, of hope and of healing, his nephew had been getting sicker and sicker.

Sick enough, apparently, to require a trip to the emergency room.

It was a reminder, stark and brutal, of what was real, of how quickly everything could change and of how what you loved most could be snatched away from you. That was reality.

What was not reality was the way he felt after he had showed his soul to Stacy. It was not the laughter that had entered his life since she had been here.

It was not snowmen and snowball fights, home-made cookies, bikinis in hot springs.

Reality was a man who was not in control of any of the things he wanted to be in control of. The way he had felt, carrying her the last few yards, strong and able to protect her with his life if need be, was the biggest illusion of all.

He was not Samson.

Because he did not have the strength to say yes

to any of this again. To be open to the caprice of fate and chance.

That's what love did, in the end—it made a man's life uncertain. It left his heart wide open to the unbearable pain of loss.

He took the note and shoved it in his pocket. He went through the house and found the phone and dialed Adele's number.

"Everything okay?" he asked when she answered. He was aware he was bracing himself for the worst.

"Everything's fine," she said, and the air went out of him like a man who had dodged a bullet whistling by his ear. "The doctor says Max has an ear infection. They're keeping an eye on him for a bit, but it looks like he'll be released in about an hour."

Relief welled up in him. "That's good," he said in a calm voice that gave away nothing of the precipice he felt he had just stood on. "How did you get to the hospital?"

Better to deal with details and logistics than that uncontrollable helpless feeling that came with loving someone.

"I took a cab. I'm going to rent a car, and go

home. I think Max needs to be at home. How was your day?" she asked. "Did you have fun?"

And he heard it in her. Hope for him. And the one thing he did not want to do was give anyone false hopes. Not her.

And certainly not Stacy.

"I'll come get you," he told his sister. "I'll drive you home."

"But what about Stacy?"

He said nothing.

"Oh, Kiernan," she said, her voice part annoyance and part sympathy. "Don't throw this away."

He ended the call without responding to that. Stacy was in the kitchen putting on a kettle. For a moment his resolve wavered. He could picture them sitting together having hot chocolate. Max wasn't here. He could build a fire in the hearth without concerns for the baby's safety.

It felt, for a moment, as if he could picture their whole lives together…for a moment he could see this room the way she had seen it the first time she had entered…full of laughter and family, a big Christmas tree and toys on the floor.

And he steeled himself against the yearning that vision caused in him.

"How is Max?" she asked anxiously.

"It's an ear infection. He's being released in an hour or so. I'm going to go get them."

"All right." She had heard something in his tone. He could see his coolness register on her face. "Do you want me to come with you?"

It felt like that *no* was the hardest thing he'd ever said. But no, there was something harder yet that had to be said, that had to be done.

She had to know there was no hope. Not for them. None.

"I'll go back to the city with them," he said. "I won't be coming back here."

"Oh! I'll get my things, then. And clear out, too."

"I'll need your contact information."

Hope flickered briefly until she registered how he had worded that. Not *I'll call*. Not *I'll be in touch.*

"My lawyer will contact you," he said, struggling to strip all emotion from his voice. "I'll want you to sign something saying the things we have discussed were in strictest confidence."

It did exactly as he had both hoped and dreaded it would do.

It shattered her.

She turned swiftly from him and unplugged the kettle. She went through the drawers until she found a piece of paper and a pen.

She wrote her information down, her curls falling like a curtain in front of her face. He didn't stay to watch. He went to his room and shut the door. He did not come out until he heard the front door close behind her.

He ordered himself not to look, but he went to the front window anyway and watched her drive away.

Then he went and retrieved the information from where she had left it on the counter. He unfolded the piece of paper.

Written on it was not her mailing address or her phone number or her email.

Written on it in unhesitating script, it read, *"Go to hell."*

And despite the pain he was in, he could not help but smile. Because, unlike him, Stacy Murphy Walker had long ago learned to roll with the punches.

He crumpled up the paper and threw it on the counter. He went and looked at the guest room.

There was nothing in there to show she had ever been there. The faint smell of lemons and soap would not be here by the next time he came back. The fountain she had toppled would be righted, eventually, and the shrubs replanted.

Probably all that would happen before he came back here, because he was not at all sure when that would be.

Wouldn't this place, now, be forever connected in his mind to her?

All he had left of her was a wet bathing suit in his backpack. A bathing suit Adele might want back.

And then in a moment that he recognized as utter weakness, he went back into the kitchen, picked Stacy's note up off the counter and straightened the crumples out of it with his fist. He folded it carefully and put it in his shirt pocket.

He wanted to keep something of her. Even if it was this.

Maybe especially if it was this. Something that showed him, after all, that she was strong. And spunky. She was going to be fine.

He was just not so sure about himself.

CHAPTER SEVENTEEN

STACY MURPHY WALKER would have been stunned to know that Kiernan McAllister thought she would be fine. She was not fine.

She cried for a week. She screamed into her pillow. She didn't get dressed. Or comb her hair. She didn't brush her teeth or pick up her newspapers from the front door.

She made cookies and ate them all to prove cookies tasted just as good without him in her life. She drank a bucket of hot chocolate just to reassure herself that it was still good.

But the truth was, the cookies tasted like sawdust and the hot chocolate might as well have been bathwater.

A few days with him, and she was reacting like this! With more drama and heartache and grief than the end of her six-month courtship with Dylan. It was shameful! She was lucky it had only been a few days with him! Imagine if it had been longer? Imagine if they had let that kiss get away from them? Then what would she be feeling?

Though, in truth, she wondered if she could possibly be feeling any worse!

This seemed like a preview of her future life: drab and tasteless, unexciting. The potential for it to be something else had shimmered briefly and enticingly, and now that was gone.

At the end of a full week of immersion in her misery, Stacy knew she had to pull herself together. She had bills to pay! Other people might have the luxury of wallowing in a heartbreak but she did not!

Murphy's Law once again: everything that could go wrong, had. Why should she be surprised? It was the story of her life, after all.

And there was a positive side: nothing could steal those moments from her. Nothing could take the memories of her snow angel, and their snowball fight, the snowman that might still be melting in his yard. Nothing could take the ski trip and that beautiful little cabin and those moments in the hot tub, where it had seemed, for one shining instant, as if the events of all her life had led her to *this*.

"Stop it," she ordered herself. It was her imagination, run wild again, that had got her in all this trouble.

Had she actually talked herself into believing a man like Kiernan McAllister could feel anything for her?

She snorted her self-disgust out loud.

Then, newly determined, Stacy went and gathered the newspapers from her front door and went through them, one by one, looking for the lead that would launch her new career as a freelancer.

But nothing in the business section interested her.

In fact, if she was really honest about it, business had *never* interested her. In a moment of desperation, with no funds to complete college, she had taken the first job that had been offered to her. Fallen into it, really.

And if she looked at her failed relationship with Dylan, it had the same hallmarks: the relationship had presented itself to her. She had fallen into it rather than chosen it. She had been flattered by his attention. It had been convenient. It had seemed like the easiest route to what she wanted: to feel that sense of home again.

And then she had made the same mistake with Kiernan, skidded into his life instead of choosing it for herself.

"That's done," she told herself firmly. "Falling into things is done. My life happening by accident is done."

Stacy set down the papers. She got out her laptop.

What did she want to write about? If she was going to steer into the spin instead of away from it, what story would she tell? Asking herself that question seemed to open a floodgate.

A week later she sold the piece to *Pacific Life* magazine for more money than she had ever expected. The article sparked interest in her charity the likes of which she had not seen before.

Some of the kids she worked with had seen the piece, and they wanted to write their stories.

She started a blog for them. *Pacific Life* picked up some of stories.

Speaking invitations began to roll in. Stacy

began to have a life she had never dreamed possible.

And if it was missing one thing, she tried not to think about that.

It was only at night, when another hectic day had ended, and her head was on the pillow, that she would let herself think of those fewdays of wonder.

And the newest success story in Vancouver would cry herself to sleep.

Adele walked into Kiernan's apartment as if she owned the place. She looked around as if she was going to set Max down, but what she saw must have made her think better of it.

Kiernan glared at her. The apartment was dark, and he was sitting on the couch, remote control for the TV in his hand. He muted the sound on the television. "What are you doing here? And how did you get in?"

She wagged a key at him. "I got it from the apartment manager. I said I was conducting a well-being check."

"He fell for that?"

"Women with babies are nearly always perceived as trustworthy."

"I'm going to see that he's fired."

Adele made a sucking sound through her teeth. He never liked it when she made that sound. It never boded well for him.

"God, where's your housekeeper?"

"I fired her."

"Well, it smells in here."

"I burned the pizza."

"You tried to make your own pizza?"

She said that as if it told her a deep dark secret about him. And maybe it did. He had tried to cook pizza in an effort to prove to himself he could have the very same life without Stacy that he could have with her. The experiment had been a dismal failure, but apparently, from the look on Adele's face, she already knew that.

"Did you fire your housekeeper before or after you fired Miss Harris?" Adele asked.

"I hired her back! Where did you hear I fired Miss Harris?"

"Mark told me."

"Well, tell him he can be fired, too. What happens at the office stays at the office."

"Look, brother dear, you can fire everyone you come in contact with, but it's obviously not going to make you feel any better."

"It does make me feel better," he insisted, watching her darkly.

"You have to deal with what's at the heart of the matter, Kee."

"And I suppose you know what that is?" he snarled.

"Of course I do!"

He cocked his head at her, raised an eyebrow.

"Your heart," she said. "Your heart is at the heart of that matter."

Her eyes, unfortunately, seemed to be adjusting to the dark in here, because she picked her way through the dirty socks and shirts on the floor and stood over him. Max peeked at him and apparently didn't like what he saw—or feared being left again—because he nuzzled into his mother's shoulder and sucked feverishly on his thumb.

Adele reached down and picked up a magazine off a heap of them on the coffee table.

"What's this?"

"Don't touch that!"

"*Icons of Business.* Haven't you been featured

in this?" When he didn't answer, she frowned. "Good grief, Kee, are you ego-surfing through your glory days?"

"You're saying that as if they are in the past," he said, increasingly annoyed at this invasion into his misery, wanting to deflect her from seeing why he was really surrounded by several years of issues of *Icons of Business.*

She was juggling Max, flipping through the magazine, obviously totally looking in the wrong direction, thinking she would find a story about him.

Then, to his chagrin, a light went on in her face. "Oh my God, you are reading all Stacy's stories!"

She said that as if he was being adorable.

"I'm gathering ammunition to help me prepare the lawsuit when she writes the unauthorized story about me!"

It was weak and not credible and he knew it.

"You'll be preparing your own lawsuit, I guess, since you fired Harry last week?"

He didn't even ask her where she had heard that. He hoped his glare balanced out the flimsy explanation of why he was reading Stacy's writing enough to make his sister stop talking and leave. Apparently it didn't.

"She's not going to write about you, silly."

"Silly?"

"I had coffee with her. After I saw the article she wrote in *Pacific Life.*"

"You had coffee with Stacy? Last week?" He had to bite his tongue to keep from asking all the questions that wanted to tumble off it. *Was she okay? Was she happy? Did she ask about him?*

Instead he asked, "What was the article about?"

"Not you." She let that sink in, just to let him know the whole world was not about him.

"Is there a point to this visit? Oh, just a sec. Well-being check. You can clearly see I'm alive, so—"

"I brought you a copy to look at." Still juggling the baby, she put down the copy of *Icons of Business* and fished around in a purse enormous enough to hold a Volkswagen. She found what she wanted and put it on top of his mess on the coffee table.

"Why?"

"Oh, quit snarling. Because I love you, and care

about you and trust that after you have read it you will still know how to do the right thing."

He decided, stubbornly, even before his sister left, that he was *never* reading the article. He made it for twenty minutes, pretending interest in the football game his sister had so rudely interrupted.

But he was once again, Samson, sans hair. He had no strength.

He picked up the magazine and flipped through it until he found the article that Stacy had written. It was called "Murphy's Law: Confessions of a Foster Child," and it started with the words, *I believed in magic until I was sixteen years old...*

When he finished it, he read it again. He was aware his face was wet with tears.

And he was aware of something else. His sister was right. He still did know how to do the right thing.

And somehow finding his checkbook in this mess he had created of his life and writing a big fatty to CCOFK was not going to cut it.

By the time he had finished reading that story, he knew what he had always known in his heart. He knew exactly who Stacy was.

But he knew something beyond that, too. And it was something that could change his life and lead him out of darkness if he had the courage to embrace it.

CHAPTER EIGHTEEN

STACY WAS BEYOND EXHAUSTED. Her life had taken off in so many unexpected directions in the past few weeks! Though she had sworn her cookie-and-hot-chocolate days were over, it did sound like an easy supper after a long, hard day. And she was putting on her pajamas to eat it, too.

Her doorbell rang and she went to it, in her pajamas, cookies in hand. She peeked out the side window and reeled away, her back against the door.

Her heart was beating too fast.

Just as if it might explode.

She was not opening that door. She was not. She had cookies melting in her hands. She was in her pajamas at seven o'clock at night. Her hair was a mess, and she had already wiped all the makeup off her face.

In her imagination, she had pictured seeing him again, down to the last detail. She had thought maybe their paths would cross at a charity function. And that she would be wearing designer clothes and Kleinback shoes. Her hair would be upswept, her makeup perfect, and she would be sipping very expensive champagne.

Nothing, she thought, a touch sourly, *ever goes the way I plan it.*

He knocked again. She was not going to open that door. But she could not resist putting her eye to a little slit in the drapery to have one last look at him.

Kiernan McAllister did not look anything like he did in her imaginings. In fact, he looked awful! His face was whisker roughened like it had been the first day she saw him. His hair hadn't been cut recently, and it was touching his collar.

He was not dressed in one of the custom suits that he always wore when he graced the cover of a magazine.

Or in the casuals he had worn at his cottage.

He was in a thin windbreaker that wasn't warm enough for the blustery Vancouver day. His jeans had a hole in the knee.

But it was his eyes that made her fling open the door.

They had dark circles under them. The light in them was haunted.

"Hello," she said. She took a bite of her cookie to make sure he did not have a clue her heart was beating so fast it might explode at any second.

"Hello, Murphy."

Her defenses were down quite enough without him calling her that.

"How have you been?" he asked softly.

As if he really cared.

"All right," she said. She took another bite of the cookie and hoped to hell she wouldn't choke on it. "You?"

It was ludicrous, them standing there asking each other these banal questions as if they had bumped into each other on the street.

"I haven't been doing so good," he said.

She gave up all pretense of eating the cookie and really looked at him. It felt as if her heart were breaking in two.

"Can I come in?" he said. "I really need to talk to you."

Did he have to? Come in? To her space? It wasn't that it was humble, because it was, and that did not embarrass her in the least.

It was that once he had been in here, some part of him would linger forever. She would never feel the same way about her space again.

Still, she stood back from the door.

He came by her and looked around, a little smile playing around the edge of his mouth.

"What?"

"It's just as I imagined."

"*You* imagined where *I* live?"

"I did," he confessed. He took off his coat and, seeing no place to hang it, put it on the doorknob.

She watched him go and flop down on her couch. He closed his eyes, like a man gathering himself.

Or like a man who had found his way home.

"How did you imagine it?" she asked.

"Like something I saw in a children's book a long time ago—a little rabbit warren, safe and full of color and coziness and those little touches that make a house into a home. Like this." He picked up a doily on her coffee table.

"Why are you here?" she asked, and she could hear something plaintive in her voice that begged him to put her out of her misery.

He patted the spot on the couch beside him.

She hesitated, but she could not say no. She went and sat beside him. The couch was not large enough to leave as much space between them as she would have liked. Her shoulder was nearly brushing his. She could feel the heat and energy pulsating off him. His scent tickled her nostrils, clean and tantalizingly masculine.

"I always thought I was a courageous man," he said, his voice soft. "When I was swooping down mountains where no one had ever skied before, when I was jumping out of airplanes, when I was zip-lining through the jungle, I was always congratulating myself on what a brave guy I was."

She said nothing, but she felt herself move, fractionally, closer to him.

"Of course, I wasn't at all," he said slowly. "I was just filling up all the empty spaces in my life with one adrenaline rush after another. I was outrunning something, even before Danner died."

She shifted again until their shoulders were touching lightly.

"I was outrunning the thing that took the most courage of all. I was terrified of it. I had experienced its treachery, and I couldn't trust it.

"And when Danner died, I took it as proof that I was right."

"Love," she said, her voice choked, her shoulder and his leaning against each other, supporting each other. "It's love that takes the most courage."

"Yes, love."

The way he said the word, love could be taken two ways, one of them as an endearment.

"But the thing I was running hardest from is the thing that will be brought to you again and again. It's like the universe cannot accept no as an answer to that one thing.

"And so love tracks you down. In a baby whose laughter could make a heart of stone come back to life. In a sister who is so brokenhearted and who needs you to man up.

"In a woman who crashes into your fountain, and announces to you, who already knows, that anything that can go wrong will."

"How can you love me?" Stacy whispered.

"I didn't say I loved you."

"Oh," she said, not even trying to hide how crushed that made her feel.

He turned his face to hers, put a finger under her chin and tilted it up to him. "I said I had been brought the opportunity to say yes to love. You see, Murphy, that's why I'm here."

"Why?"

"To see if you can teach me about real courage. You're right. I don't know if I love you. But I have this feeling that I could. And it terrifies me."

"I have nothing to teach you," she whispered.

"Yes, you do." His finger was still under her chin, and he was still gazing into her eyes. After a long time, he said, "I read your article."

"You did?"

"And it's all there. Everything that you are. But maybe, Stacy, writing, at its best and its highest, does not just show who the writer is. Maybe it shows the reader who they are, too. For the first time in a long time, I feel as if I know," he said. "I know exactly who I am."

Stacy looked at him.

And she knew, too. She knew exactly who Kiernan McAllister was. And for the first time in a long, long time, she began to smile, and the smile felt as brilliant and as warm as the sun coming out after a snowstorm.

CHAPTER NINETEEN

WHEN KIERNAN MCALLISTER first began to woo Stacy Murphy Walker, he did it the way he did everything else. He went flat out and over the top. He wanted this woman to know that he meant business.

And so he chartered a chopper and had a white tablecloth dinner for her on a mountaintop, complete with white-gloved, black-suited waiters.

He took her on the company's jet for a weekend of theater and shopping and exploring in New York City.

Kiernan showered Stacy with gifts and baubles and flowers.

He took her to the most select restaurants in Vancouver. He took her to his exclusive fitness club with its climbing wall, indoor pool and steam room.

Her first time downhill skiing was at Steamboat in Colorado, with him by her side.

In other words, he treated her the way he had treated all the other women he had ever dated.

And all those brand-new experiences delighted her, and he enjoyed them more than he ever had, experiencing them anew by running them through the filter of her complete wonder.

But it quickly became apparent to him that Stacy was not like anyone he had ever dated before.

Because while her enjoyment of each of the experiences was genuine, it became more and more apparent to Kiernan that it was when Stacey suggested how they would spend time together that they had the most fun.

Not only had the most fun but really started to get to know each other, on a different level, on a deeper level.

Stacy's idea of a good time was popcorn and a movie in her cozy little Kitsilano basement suite. Stacy's idea of a good time was a long walk, hand in hand along a deserted, windy stretch of beach. Stacy's idea of a good time was a game of Scrabble and a cup of hot chocolate.

One of her favorite things was babysitting Max so that Adele and Mark, who had slipped away quietly to the Bahamas and gotten married, could have some grown-up time together.

Because of that Kiernan got used to eating hamburgers under the Golden Arches and puzzling together the toy that came in the kid's meal. Because of that he got used to visiting the aquarium and going to story time at the library.

"He's not old enough for story time," he had protested when she first suggested it.

And then been proved wrong when the wriggly little Max had sat still as a stone as the librarian read a picture book.

Because of that, he got used to the park, and pushing a stroller, and visiting the pet store and fishing kids' music CDs out of the player in his car. Because of that he knew all about the elf on the shelf, and he knew who Thomas and Dora were.

Stacy's idea of a good time was serving Christmas dinner to her "kids." Her idea of a good time was being able to organize a day of skiing for those foster kids, or a picnic or a day of swimming.

More and more, Kiernan was aware that Stacy's idea of a good time was often intrinsically intertwined with helping others.

And somehow, he had become involved in that, too. Those kids she introduced him to, the ones in foster care, were so much like his younger self.

But today, Kiernan had chosen what they were doing. He was leading the way to Last Chance. There had been no early snowstorm this year, and so they were hiking up there to what had become one of their favorite places on earth.

"So beautiful," Stacy said, shrugging off her pack.

He was already being distracted by thoughts of what bathing suit she might have brought.

She seemed distracted by food. Getting out the hot dogs, and buns and marshmallows and, as had become their tradition, a very expensive bottle of ice wine.

Later, in the hot pool, with the steam rising around them, he looked at her and thought she was the most beautiful woman he had ever seen.

She was leaning back in the water, her eyes closed, her hair floating around her, her face tranquil.

But he didn't feel tranquil. He was not sure he,

who had defied death with countless feats of daring, had ever felt more nervous in his whole life.

"Stacy?"

She turned and looked at him, righted herself. Something in his face must have told her something very, very important was going on. She came over to him and wrapped her arms around him, looked up into his face.

"What is it, Kiernan? Is something wrong?"

Yes, something was wrong. He hadn't planned to do this in the hot pool. The ring was in the backpack inside the cabin.

He swallowed hard. "Do you know what day it is?" he asked her.

She looked puzzled. "October twenty-sixth?"

He nodded, and could not speak past the lump in his throat.

"Oh, no," she whispered. "It's the anniversary of Danner's death, isn't it? Oh, Kiernan."

And then she said, "Oh, gosh, we should be with Adele."

"It's not," he said. "It's not the anniversary of Danner's death."

Though that day was coming, he recognized,

a little shocked, it was not the raw, open wound it had been just a year ago.

"Then what day is it?" she asked. "What is wrong with you?"

"It's a year to the day since you chugged up my driveway and slid into my fountain."

"Oh!" she said.

"It's a year to the day since my life began to change forever. For the better. In ways I could not have imagined. I have something I want to tell you."

"What?" she whispered.

"I'm going to leave McAllister Enterprises."

Did she look disappointed? Yes, she did. He could thank his lucky stars, he supposed, that he hadn't cracked open the wine yet, or he might be wearing it!

"With your blessing," he continued, watching her closely, "I want to turn running it completely over to Mark."

Had she been expecting a proposal? If she had, she seemed to be getting over her disappointment a little too quickly.

"But it's your life!" she said. "Your baby. You

started that company. You took it to where it is today."

"It was only a step in the road," he said. "It was only to give me the skills I need to do something else."

"But what?"

He took a deep breath. "I feel as if my whole life has been leading me to this," he told her, the person he could tell anything to. "My whole life, every triumph, and every tragedy, too, has led me to this moment, and this decision."

He felt how right this was.

Will you marry me?

But he made himself wait.

"I want take on Career and College Opportunities for Foster Kids. Stacy, that group is getting ready to explode. It's ready to become more than a tiny charity in Vancouver. It needs to go North America wide."

He could tell she was excited, and disappointed, too. He would play her just a little while longer, the anticipation building in him.

"I want to be at the helm when that happens," he told her, having trouble concentrating on what he was saying. "I want to guide it through its infancy. I have an opportunity to do so much for those young people. Working with it has given my life meaning like nothing else, except..."

He looked at her.

She was holding her breath. She knew what was coming. She had to.

He felt his heart swell inside him. He felt the light dancing with any darkness that remained within him, dancing until they all swirled together and became one magnificent, glorious thing.

"...except you," he said quietly. "Stacy, I don't want to take it on by myself. I want you at my side."

"Of course," she whispered, tears running down her beautiful cheeks.

"I don't just want you at my side to take CCOFK to the next level. I want you at my side for everything. Stacy, I want you to marry me. I want you to be my wife."

For a full minute, she tilted back her head and stared at up him as if she could not comprehend what he had just said, as if maybe she had not expected this after all.

And then she let out a whoop of pure joy that

said everything about what she had become in this past year.

Love, he could see, had taken her to the next level.

He was not sure he had ever been in the presence of such pure joy as Stacy radiated an unbelievable enthusiasm for life, an ability to embrace each day as an adventure.

"Will you marry me?"

Kiernan had thought he would be down on one knee, with the ring extended, but he could see that now, as always, when he let go of control just a little bit, life had a better plan for him than anything he could plan for himself.

Because he knew he would remember this moment, in its absolute perfection, forever.

"Yes!" she cried.

And the mountains rang with her joy and echoed that yes back to him as he picked her up and swung her around in the warm steamy water and then kissed her face all over as if he could never, ever get enough of her.

"Yes," she whispered. "Yes, yes, yes."

EPILOGUE

THE MOUNTAIN TRAIL was beautiful in the spring-time. The trees were breaking out in tender, lime-green leaves; the grass shoots were young and fragile, and the moss along the path was like velvet under Stacy Murphy Walker's feet.

Kiernan had said he would deliver her by helicopter, but she'd said no. If her life had taught her anything, it was that it was the journey that mattered, not the arrival.

This day was like nothing she had ever imagined, she thought, as she came into the clearing of the little cabin, Last Chance.

The clearing was full of people. The chairs and the pagoda and the tent for the reception festivities afterward had all been delivered by helicopter.

She was in a long white dress, and a cheer went up when people saw her come from the forest. She walked down the aisle, lifted her skirt to let everyone see her hiking boots and was rewarded with laughter.

Waiting, under that pagoda, was Kiernan, his eyes soft on her, a look in them better, so much better, than anything Stacy could have ever imagined.

Oh, everything that could go wrong had. The minister had suffered a bee sting and been airlifted out with one of the supply helicopters. A new official had been found at the last minute—Kiernan's amazing staff, especially Miss Harris, could do anything.

One of the food boxes had been dropped—from a considerable height—and naturally, it was the one that had contained the cake.

Adele had been in charge of the wedding band, and she had turned away from Max for just one second, and turned back to find the jewelry box empty, the ring nowhere to be found and Max looking innocent as could be.

All of those mishaps seemed fairly minor, even comic, to Stacy. One thing about living a life where things tended to go wrong? You developed a certain grace for dealing with it.

Now, as she walked toward the man who would

be her husband, all of it faded: the little cabin and the turquoise waters of the spring that bubbled behind it, Max throwing a tantrum because his mother and Mark were at the front and he was not.

All of it faded: the tent that she passed that was as exquisitely set up as if they were having their wedding at the finest hotel instead of in the wilderness; their guests, some of them dabbing at their eyes as she passed them, doing her little heel kick with the hiking boots.

All of it faded, except him.

Her beloved. Kiernan.

She came to a stop before him, and he reached for her, and their hands joined, and their eyes remained on each other, never straying as they exchanged those age-old words:

In sickness and in health,
In good times and in bad,
In joy as well as in sorrow...

It seemed to Stacy that Kiernan's voice rose out of the mountains themselves, it was so strong and so sure as he spoke the final vow to her.

"Stacy Murphy Walker, I will honor and respect you. I will laugh with you and I will cry with you. I will cherish you, for as long as we both shall live."

When his lips claimed hers, the world, despite the great cheer from the onlookers, went silent.

And when she stepped back and looked into his silvery eyes, Stacy felt a deep truth within herself.

It was the truth that was stated in those simple vows they had just spoken.

There would be moments like this and many of them—moments of genuine and complete bliss.

But even the wedding vows made room for Murphy! In health *and* in sickness, in good times *and* in bad, in joy *and* in sorrow…

And all lightness aside, as she looked into her new husband's eyes, this was the truth that Stacy Murphy Walker McAllister stood in.

It was not the triumphs that shaped the human race. It was not these moments of temporary bliss that were gone in a second or an hour or a day, and that left people in the everlasting pursuit of *more*.

No, these moments were the gift at the end of the long hard climb, like reaching the mountaintop after climbing the long, rocky trail. Only you didn't get to stay there, on top of the world, drinking in the glory and the magnificence forever. No, eventually, you had to eat and sleep and get some clean clothes and brush your teeth. Eventually, you went back down the mountain to the valley that was life.

To the rainy days and the kids crying, to burned cookies and a fender-bender, and maybe a career disappointment or a goal not reached. Eventually you went back down the mountain to a life that was real.

And in that life that was real, Stacy felt it was tragedies that truly shaped people.

It was the breakdown of a relationship.

It was the death of a parent.

It was watching helplessly as someone you loved struggled with an unexpected illness.

It was an able-bodied person becoming disabled.

It was the business decision gone sour.

It was the friendship betrayed.

It was a parent, for reasons real or imagined, cut from a child's life.

These were the things that shaped people forever, what made them who they really were. These were the things that asked them to be stronger, more compassionate and more forgiving than they ever thought they were capable of being.

It was in these moments of utter defeat and utter despair, these moments of absolute blackness, when a person cast their glance heavenward, toward the light.

It was in these moments, where a person found their knees and whispered that plea of one who had been humbled by life and struggled with darkness—*help me.*

And that plea, if you listened carefully and with a heart wide open, was answered with, *how will you handle this?*

How will you use this, your worst moment, your heartbreak, your disappointment, your tragedy— how will you use this in service?

And sometimes if you were very lucky, or very blessed, as Stacy Murphy Walker McAllister had been, as Kiernan had been, you were allowed to stand in the light, in a moment of complete grace, when you could see.

When you could see who you really were.

And when you could see who your beloved really was.

And then you could sigh with contentment and proclaim it all, every single bit of it, light and darkness, and especially love, to be good.

* * * * *

Mills & Boon® Large Print
January 2015

1214 Rom LP

MILLS & BOON®
Large Print – February 2015

AN HEIRESS FOR HIS EMPIRE
Lucy Monroe

HIS FOR A PRICE
Caitlin Crews

COMMANDED BY THE SHEIKH
Kate Hewitt

THE VALQUEZ BRIDE
Melanie Milburne

THE UNCOMPROMISING ITALIAN
Cathy Williams

PRINCE HAFIZ'S ONLY VICE
Susanna Carr

A DEAL BEFORE THE ALTAR
Rachael Thomas

THE BILLIONAIRE IN DISGUISE
Soraya Lane

THE UNEXPECTED HONEYMOON
Barbara Wallace

A PRINCESS BY CHRISTMAS
Jennifer Faye

HIS RELUCTANT CINDERELLA
Jessica Gilmore

MILLS & BOON®

Why shop at millsandboon.co.uk?

Each year, thousands of romance readers find their perfect read at millsandboon.co.uk. That's because we're passionate about bringing you the very best romantic fiction. Here are some of the advantages of shopping at www.millsandboon.co.uk:

* **Get new books first**—you'll be able to buy your favourite books one month before they hit the shops

* **Get exclusive discounts**—you'll also be able to buy our specially created monthly collections, with up to 50% off the RRP

* **Find your favourite authors**—latest news, interviews and new releases for all your favourite authors and series on our website, plus ideas for what to try next

* **Join in**—once you've bought your favourite books, don't forget to register with us to rate, review and join in the discussions

Visit **www.millsandboon.co.uk**
for all this and more today!